Way Down Deep

CHARLOTTE STEIN
& CARA McKENNA

First Edition

Edited by Ruth Homrighaus

Cover design by Cara McKenna

Formatting by Vellum

ISBN: 978-0-9980911-3-6

With our deepest thanks to Ruth and Molly,
trusted midwives at the birth of our wonky baby.
And as always, thank you, lovely readers.

WAY DOWN DEEP

FRIDAY

Unknown Number

3.03am

I know it's pointless, writing to you. I know you won't text back.

But I've been stuffing everything down for so long, if I don't put it into words it's going to rot me from the inside out.

This town's the size of a mud puddle, but it still feels like I'm drowning here. Drowning in strangers. Drowning in silence, more than anything else.

Drowning doesn't even sound that bad, some days. People say suicide is the coward's way out, but is it? Doing nothing is cowardly. Suicide takes action.

Jesus, this is so pathetic. Thank fuck you'll never actually read this. Anyhow. Goodnight, wherever you are.

SATURDAY

1.46am

I've rewrote this text fifty times, and gone back and forth on whether to reply about a million times more. Even now I've got no clue whether I should be saying something—because I'm not the person you want to talk to. I don't know who this person is or whether they care or not but I can tell you this:

I care. I care about you, stranger. At least enough to try throwing you a life jacket before your head disappears beneath the water line.

Yeah, suicide does take action.

But staying afloat takes more when you've got nothing to hold onto.

So just grab a hold of this, okay?

SUNDAY

9.10am

Oh my god, I'm SO sorry. This used to be someone else's number.

That's super fucked up, that I probably woke you with all that psycho sad sack bullshit at 3am. You were really kind to reply, but don't waste any more time worrying about me. I probably drank a little more than I should have that night.

I'm okay, really. Just feeling sorry for myself. Though now I feel like such a crazy melodramatic asshole, there's not much room left over for self-pity. I guess I have you to thank for that. So thanks, stranger.

Sorry again. I promise I'll delete this number now.

1.05pm

I just spent pretty much all morning trying to decide what to do. I'd hit on a possible answer while eating breakfast, then by the time I was done it would seem like the most foolish words that anyone has ever spoken. At one point, I even made a pros and cons list for the two main options, but still didn't really get much closer. Which sounds pretty extreme, I know, but then even the smallest answers feel dangerous.

I mean, I could say you don't seem melodramatic. But what if that makes you slide back into the water? And if I say you did, I'm definitely going to be that arsehole who rolls their eyes and jokes about people who are depressed.

So in the end, I thought I'd skip out on both and choose option three:

Don't delete my number.

Or at least, don't delete it because you think you bothered me. Even if expressing depressed feelings falls into that category, I'm never doing anything that you could possibly interrupt. As we speak, I'm sprawled on my couch in pyjamas I've yet to change out of, while the fiftieth episode of something I'm not even watching plays on the TV.

The very worst crime you'll ever be guilty of is making me rewind something back to the beginning.

MONDAY

1.48am

I hope this won't wake you.

I hope that, yet there I went sending it anyhow. Just more fodder for my growing asshole cred.

The first time you replied I got a little freaked out, because it popped up with someone else's name. Someone who wouldn't be texting me back unless Jesus fell off the wagon and started drunkenly tossing miracles around.

Speaking of drunk, yet again I'm probably not what you'd call entirely lucid. No doubt the liquor played a part in loosening my fingers enough for one to slip and hit the send button.

All afternoon, I tried to talk myself into deleting your number, so I wouldn't wind up spraying my sad all over you again in a fit of sloppy weakness exactly like this one, but in the end I couldn't. I just changed the contact from the old name to Stranger.

Anyhow, it was nice to hear from you, stranger. Like I was shouting into the void and the void was kind enough to whisper back. The void cares more than most of my friends, as it turns out.

Also, what are you watching? I'm watching some Nazi documentary. What is it with British TV? So goddamn many Nazis.

2.58am

You don't have to worry about waking me up. Chances are you won't be. I sleep like someone trying to start an engine stuffed with sugar—in stuttery fits and starts. Really you're saving me from staring at the ceiling. Or from nightmares that are usually about me, staring at the ceiling.

Oh and I don't care if you're drunk, either. My stone-cold sober is usually weirder than most people's blotto. I mean, when you said you wanted to call me Stranger, my first response was a burst of happiness at the idea of having a secret name. How ridiculous is that?

And is it more or less ridiculous that I've already given you a secret name back? Smith, I've called you, after the author of that poem. You know the one—I was much too far out all my life, and not waving but drowning.

Hopefully that's not too pretentious. Or too much of a reminder of the miracle that isn't happening. Or the friends that aren't calling. They're all fools to not want to talk about Nazis on British TV at three in the morning, I promise.

I want to talk to you about it, and I barely know you. I don't even know where you're from. Up until this point I thought you were British, and so understood our strange ways. But now I see I will have to guide you through them. Explain in detail why we love dull-voiced documentaries about Nazis so much. Help you understand what makes them so vital to our country.

Here it is, the big revelation:

I haven't got a bloody clue.

It's as much a mystery to me as it is to you.

I don't even think I've ever watched one all the way through—right now I'm in the middle of The Killing. Give me dismembered bodies and haunted detectives and rain-drenched roads over grainy footage of Churchill any day of the goddamn week.

3.18am

Hi, stranger.

I stayed awake on the off chance you'd reply. I waited and watched that entire stupid documentary, and then there was a ping just as the credits rolled. And then another. Nine pings, and I waited for them to stop for good before I read what you wrote.

Was I afraid to interrupt you? I think maybe. Or maybe something else. Some greedy cousin of anticipation.

I held my breath and waited, waited, and the pings kept coming, like a box of chocolates filling up. It made me feel strange, and warm, like this middle-shelf bourbon is doing. Plus some other bad food-and-beverage similes I can't think of just now.

Yeah, I'm not from these parts. I'm from the States, New Mexico. It's a long story how I wound up here, in a tiny little turd of a village just off the M1. It's not quirky and picturesque and beset by a disproportionate number of murders like the British villages in the shows my aunt likes to watch on PBS. I'd kill for a murder. This place is dull as fuck.

But here I am, and here I'm stuck for the time being. It's very wet and gray. I don't mean to piss on your country, but I won't lie, it's rough. At least when you come from a place that's dry and sunny 362 days a year, it is. And if you're a whiny douche who can't handle a little rain.

I'm homesick, ignore me. Maybe only March sucks. Maybe April will be better.

Hey, look at me, the eternal optimist!

I feel like I should wonder if you're a man or a woman, if you're sixty or sixteen, but I don't really care. I think maybe you're a woman, but that's probably just me being sexist, thinking only women know about poetry or worry about strangers.

You don't have to tell me. It doesn't matter. I only care that you're a human and you're awake and you're kind, when you have no reason to be. That you said, "I'm here," when almost anybody else who got those texts would've said,

"Fuck off, stalker, wrong number." If they bothered to say anything at all.

It makes me wonder what I would've said. I feel small and a little ashamed that I can't guess.

Now me, I don't know about poetry, but that one you quoted sounds nice. I'll look it up. When I read that you think of me as Smith I first thought of Elliott Smith, because lately I've been listening to all the music that used to make depression sound so romantic, back before I knew what depression actually feels like.

I wish I had the same problems I did back then. I didn't even know what problems were, or what hopelessness is like to live inside, like a well that's so empty there's no water and no floor, not even any walls, too bottomless for you to make out the sky or stars or hear somebody calling your name. If anyone's even noticed you went missing.

Fucking similes. Hey, maybe this one makes you my bucket. Deep, right? I think I better leave the poetry to you.

I've been listening to way too much Nick Drake lately, too. He's my kind of poet. You showing up makes me think of some of his lyrics. Now you're here. Brighten my northern sky.

Before I shut the fuck up, I want to let you know, I'm not going to kill myself. I can't. I have something too important to live for.

Believe me, I fantasize about it. I fantasize that it's an option, that I could hit the stop button on the shit show my life's become, but I can't, and I won't. Promise. So don't worry. I'm here to stay.

Now try to get some sleep, stranger-bucket.

3.30am

First of all, can I just say that I love you waiting for the pings? Every time I text I get this slight sizzle of nerves that you'll want to text back the way normal people do—immediate and between the seven thousand things I want to say, instead of all slow and deliberate and like letters. I love that this is like sending each other letters.

And don't worry, I love your similes.

I'm currently rolling around in all of them, especially the chocolate one.

Though can you blame me? Now all I can think about is a hot dry place I've never been to, and the taste of middle-shelf bourbon that I'm imagining is sticky and warm, and a well that's so empty and lightless you need me to let down the rope.

I hope I'm doing it well enough. I hope you're telling the truth.

I hope the something that is too important is as cool and amazing as you sound.

You deserve amazing just for Elliot Smith. I've never heard him in my whole life—I didn't even know he existed. But now I'm lying on my bed in the dark, his words whispering over me in waves. Drink up baby, stay up all night, with the things you could do, you won't but you might…

You're probably going to tell me that they mean something specific. That they're about a girlfriend he lost to heroin or some sleazy thing he did in a bar one time. But just for right now I want to imagine those words are only for me, or for both of us, like a soundtrack to the weird conversation we seem to be slipping into.

Because this is slipping, for me.

Usually I hesitate. I bargain with my own words.

I let out two as long as ten stay behind.

Yet I don't seem to be doing that with you.

I wonder why? Part of me thinks it's because you don't know me, can't see me, aren't even aware of what gender I am. But mostly I read you saying things about suicide, and it's like you're slicing through the wall that holds back everything I would usually never say.

I would never usually say things like cool and amazing, but I don't care if it could be the last thing you ever know about yourself. All that matters is that you do know it.

Goodnight, Smith.

Sleep well, under whatever bright northern sky I provide.

10.52am

Yes, letters. You're right, that's what these are.

I read your latest one in bed just before the sun came up, and I've been turning that thought around and around all morning as I showered and made coffee and breakfast and took care of things around here.

I can't remember the last time anyone sent me a letter, or I sent one to somebody. Not even a heartfelt email. People don't really do that these days—take turns, wait for the other person to finish saying what's on their mind.

We don't tell stories about ourselves anymore, just let the mundane blurt from our brains into our phones, hit send, half-read the reply in a rush, knowing it's our turn to blurt again, to send a photo of our boring lunches or our boring faces, made very slightly less boring by the application of a colorized filter.

Anyhow, I've found that idea distracting in a nice way.

And I'm finding our correspondence very refreshing. It makes me want to wait until all the pings are in, and to read what you write, then let it settle over me before I rush to word my own reply. I haven't done that in far too long.

Anyhow. My important something, as you put it, is about as far from cool as a something can get.

That's a lesson I've been learning in recent weeks. That "important" and "cool" rarely intersect. Cool used to be a very big part of my life.

Before I moved here, I owned a liquor store. To say "liquor store" doesn't paint the right picture, though. It was a boutique, basically, in the most happening part of Albuquerque. The kind of place where parents blow $600 on a bottle of ancient Scotch to give their kid when he graduates law school, where guys my age drop ninety bucks on bourbon in an attempt to convince ourselves we're connoisseurs, not alcoholics.

I guess I'm probably a hipster. Or was. I don't have any cred anymore.

I used to, though. My shop was like hipster church. Everyone came by each week to worship and be seen and empty their wallets.

It meant a lot to me, that shop. I picked out every light fixture, stocked it with stuff you couldn't find anywhere else in the state. Hipsters fucking love hard-to-find shit, and I loved being the guy who found it.

That shop was me. It defined me the way being in a band defined me when I was in high school. I've always been like that. Like there's not enough bones and meat inside me to build a person worth knowing. Like I needed a costume as big as a whole fucking building to pass for one.

And I did pass. I had dozens of friends, all as hip and clever and unique as me. But when shit went south and I had to sell the shop, it turned out I'd picked those friends the same way I had the light fixtures. They looked good, looked right and slick and hard-to-find, but they didn't really give a shit about the guy behind the counter. They only cared about shining. Same as me.

Anyhow, that was the old me. The new me's got nothing to hide behind, just this crazy, sad, inescapable anchor keeping me here, neck-deep in my own incompetence twenty-four hours a day.

I'm no one here. I'm that sad American guy who rents the apartment above—get this—the village off-license. It's so fucking ironic, it could grace a forty-dollar T-shirt.

But that's plenty about me for now. I want to know more about you. Tell me something. Anything. You seem full inside the way I feel empty. You've got poetry for marrow and compassion pumping through your veins. You seem genuine, and earnest. Everything I'm not. So tell me how you do it, stranger.

11.45am

I think the truth is it's easy to seem full when you've spent your whole life not letting anything out. I have years of conversations inside of me; decades of unvoiced thoughts. They're practically straining at my seams. Honestly, it's a relief to have someone pluck at the stitches holding them in. To have someone actually ask about me.

I just wish there was something of worth in there to tell you. I have no interesting history—or at least nothing as interesting as hipster Scotch and fake friends and being in a band. I didn't fall from the grace of some golden false god.

There was no grace to begin with.

Only falling.

I started out above the off-license, you know? Only in my case it's above an abandoned movie theatre, after dropping out of university and dropping out of every job I've ever had and dropping out of humanity. The last time I went outside was a Tuesday, but I couldn't tell you which Tuesday it was. It could have been the last one in June.

It might have been the first one of five years ago.

Really, I'm the last person you should come to for advice on how to be a person. But if it's any consolation at all, you seem to be doing pretty good to me. You didn't have to tell me that story, but you did. And you don't have to be so honest about everything, but you are. They seem like solid places to start, if you're trying to rebuild yourself into the kind of person you want to be.

I have faith in you, Smith. Even though I've only known you for five minutes, I have faith.

Doesn't that tell you something?

12.20pm

So we're both trapped, huh?

Me by circumstances and obligation. You by…what, exactly? Something in your head? Or your past? Help me understand. What on earth could have made someone with so much to share decide to keep it all locked up?

Was it even a choice at all?

Go ahead, stranger. Break my heart. Show me I'm still capable of feeling something so tender.

12.32pm

I guess so, but I don't know if I ever thought of myself as trapped until right now. It's safe here. It's comfortable. I don't have to make any choices or decide anything in particular. The hardest part of my day is picking what to watch, what to eat, whether to get up off the couch.

I've rubbed myself a smooth, soft rut in the fabric of my life.

Though I honestly don't know why. If I did, I swear I would tell you. Nothing sounds so sweet to me as provoking tender feelings from someone who thinks he isn't capable of feeling them. But if I tried, I know I'd probably slip into lies.

Make up something juicy for you, like, "it was on the day my family died." Paint you a picture of a happy girl who lived a sunshine life, until storm cloud clichés came and stole it all away. I could describe the smell of blood with words like raw and heavy; tell you that a corpse turns the colour of spoiled food within moments.

And you would believe me.

It's just that I don't want you to.

Instead, tell me something sweet. Tell me something you like.

Tell me all your favourite things.

1.02pm

That's all I'm getting out of you, huh? You're a girl. Well, I'll settle for that if you'll tell me just one other thing about yourself…

What did you study before you dropped out of university?

As for my favorite things… Man, I've felt so little desire for anything other than sleep and whiskey these past few months, it's like I almost don't know. But for you, stranger, I'll try.

I like being barefoot. On smooth hardwood planks or warm sand or dry grass or against cool sheets. I wear socks a lot here. It's chilly and damp, and it makes my feet ache even though I'm thirty-four not seventy.

But maybe tonight after my obligations are met I'll move my chair over by the window and take off my socks and prop my feet up on the sill, just above the radiator. That might feel good.

Maybe I need to be making more of an effort to feel nice things. Instead of just trying not to feel anything at all.

What else? I like pumpkin pie. My mom made really amazing pumpkin pie from scratch, on Thanksgiving and Christmas. I'd give anything to taste that again.

I like when a bar of soap is brand new and the logo pressed into it's still crisp and you can see the seams along the sides.

I like dogs.

I like buying flowers for women.

I like music. A lot. Maybe more than anything.

I like the way my son's hair smells.

There, I said it. You're giving me crumbs, but here's the whole fucking mouse-ridden bakery for you.

I have a kid, a little boy, two and a half. I found out about him a year back, met him five months ago when I moved here because his mom's out of the picture now.

When he's not afraid of me, he's just…blank. He doesn't speak, doesn't look me or anyone except his grandmother in the eyes. He went through shit I might never know the details of, saw shit that's turned him into this frightened, silent little ghost-boy. When he's in blank-mode, I'll sit next to him while we watch TV and put my arm around him, just wait for the points where our bodies touch to grow warm, so I know he's real.

When he wakes up moaning in the middle of the night, I go to his bed and prop him up and hold him. The whiskey lets me do that. Hug him. I tell him he's safe and I'm here, and I hope my voice comforts him, the way his moans nearly comfort me, because apart from those, he never makes a sound.

I play my guitar for him, sometimes. I play Blackbird and Country Roads and Pink Moon, and I don't know if he hears.

I never wanted kids. Kids aren't cool, especially ones as damaged as this little boy, and cool used to matter so much.

The counselor I met with when I came over said to give him time, he's been through a lot. Let him know you're here, that you care, that you're not going anywhere. That you love him.

I don't know if I do, though. Love him. I want to, but how do you love someone you don't know? I have no idea what his thoughts are, because he won't talk. I have no idea if he likes my cooking, or my singing, or a toy I buy him, or if he even knows I'm his father or what that means, or trusts that I won't hurt him. He's like a wounded animal—no language, only reaction and fear.

But he's beautiful, and, yes, I like the smell of his hair at the end of the day. Even I can't find two similes to mash together to describe it. I can't say what it smells like, but it feels like coming home, somehow. Like familiarity or recognition. I knew he must be mine before the blood test results even came back, because of that smell and how exactly right it is.

He's watching TV now. I let him do that a lot, and play on my iPad, even though it can't be good for him. But it hurts too much, taking him to the park, seeing him stare fearfully at the slide and swings and pigeons like they're snarling dogs. Screens calm him, and I'm so helpless at this shit. And so fucking tired.

Okay, stranger, that was a lot. That was half of everything, so do right by me, here.

Don't tell me I'm doing great or to hang in there or that these things take time. Just tell me about you. Something real. Something solid I can dig my fingers into.

2.50pm

I can do that: I studied English Literature. Went into it expecting to meet all the friends they say you will and go to all the parties I had always missed in high school. But the friends never materialised, and I kept missing all the parties. Some because I wasn't invited. Others because I just didn't really want to go. I finally left when I realised I was only doing what I would have done anyway: devouring books and movies by the boatload.

So I understand about the nice things. I wanted them too, and I failed at getting them.

Or at least, it feels like I failed.

Sometimes I get so much joy and pleasure out of a meal or watching a movie or reading a book in the bath that I don't really know if I won or lost. I don't know if it's okay to live your life like this—through other people and places that don't actually exist. It makes me think I'll look back and wonder why I wasted all this time.

Why I didn't go barefoot while I still could.

But maybe that's silly to think, if my attempts always come to nothing?

It's hard to keep trying when it always turns out wrong. I mean, I'm utterly addicted to talking to you. Yet part of me hesitates before I pick up the phone or press send on a certain message. More and more I find myself deleting particular lines, in case those are the ones that will finally make you fall silent. Cutting myself off before you can do it for me.

I think it's why I'm not sharing as much as you might like.

Because it's easier.

It's easier to hear about you than tell you about me.

I could read about your little boy all day—it gave me a jolt of surprise and something else, something tender, just to see those words. To see you being so honest about your feelings towards him. Everyone always makes it seem terrible, to doubt whether you love a child. But love isn't something that can simply bend around all barriers. It isn't a coat you can wear for all occasions.

It's messy and elusive and strange. It runs when you think it should be there and comes when you least expect it to call. Sometimes it hits you in a rush; other times it creeps up like a thief in the night. Lies waiting for that moment when you need it most.

Or at least, I hope so.

Don't you?

6.46pm

Are you there, stranger?

The sun's setting, and I still have my socks on. The boy should be going to bed soon, though, and after that I promise my bare feet will be propped above the radiator.

Maybe I'll read a book tonight instead of watching TV. It's been a long time since I heard that sound—the dry hush of pages turning in a quiet room. I've been avoiding the quiet.

The boy gives me too much of it. Probably half of why hearing your pings coming through feels so damn nourishing.

You said, "More and more I find myself deleting particular lines, in case those are the ones that will finally make you fall silent."

It's funny, because after I sent my last messages, I told myself, if she pussies out and turns this back on me, I'm gonna be a dick. I was frustrated by some shit this afternoon, nothing to do with you. You're the one good thing right now. But I thought, if she holds back, I'm gonna say to her, tell me something goddamn real about yourself or I'm out.

That's unfair.

It's true, but it's not fair.

Because you didn't sign up for this. I was thinking before, this is so random. This is like accidental Chat Roulette. Was Chat Roulette a thing in the UK?

Basically the idea behind it was that you went on this video-chat app and you got linked up with some other user, totally random. In theory it was a beautiful thing, like some great-grandma from Corsica gets connected with a disaffected skateboarder from New Jersey, and everyone discovers they're not so different after all. Kumbaya.

But like all great things, dudes ruined it by waving their dicks around. I heard that like 99% of the time you'd wind up with a screen full of some rando jacking it.

Anyhow, I was thinking you and me, we're like Chat Roulette in the wild. But when I think harder about it, we're not. Because you didn't ask for this. You didn't sign up and hit Connect or Chat or whatever the fuck the button's labeled. I barged in like a drunk stumbling into your living room, and you were nice enough to rub my back while I puked in your flowerpots.

So yeah, that wasn't fair, my thinking you owe me a goddamn thing. You've offered up more than anybody could be expected to.

But that doesn't change how it felt, getting to hear about you. You didn't give me much, but I sucked it down like the whiskey I'm telling myself I won't drink tonight after the boy goes to bed.

Tell me a little more. Please. Tell me what you'd eat, if you could eat anything, and what you'd watch while you savored every bite. What you'd read in the tub afterward. What you'll think about while you lie in bed or on the couch or the roof or wherever it is you don't sleep at three in the morning.

(And so you know, it's never too late to go barefoot. Even if you die tomorrow, there's always tonight.)

As for me, I'm eating rice, all cheesy with broccoli. The boy seems to like it.

Normally he eats exactly three bites of whatever I put in front of him and that's it, he just quietly sets his fork down and stares at the rest while it congeals until I take it away. He's real skinny, with a big head full of the same blond curls I had when I was his age, before my hair turned brown.

His grandma—his mom's mom—told me he'll only eat these salty-as-fuck microwave noodle packets, and she gave me like twenty of them, but fuck that. I can't do much for this kid, but I can at least try to get some real food into him.

Anyhow, I made us brown rice with cheddar cheese and butter and broccoli, and he's still eating it, a fork in one hand and the other swiping at the iPad. It sounds like nothing, but I feel like Rocky standing at the top of those steps.

Fuck, I'm so tired. Tell me more if you're ready, stranger. Don't delete a thing. Don't censor yourself.

Show me all your soft, bruised, homely parts, because that's all I'm made of anymore. That's all I've got, and frankly that's all I want to see. I spent thirty-four years only caring about facades, and shock of shocks, it left me hollow.

So fill me up.

TUESDAY

6.33am

I thought about your last words way too much. In fact, I spent so long thinking how to reply that I fell asleep at an odd time, and woke up at an even odder time, and now six in the morning feels like one in the afternoon.

Though at least I now know how I feel about your words. Truth is, I kind of want you to be a dick about it. It's a novelty to have someone be a dick about me not giving enough, rather than a dick because I'm giving too much. The conversations I do remember from college were all me boring people to death, then falling silent over a hint of disinterest. I would listen to stories about other people's lives for hours, just to avoid seeming selfish or like I was monopolising things.

So you'll see a lot of me trying not to be a monopoly.

Trying not to take up too much space, or semi-apologising for spilling my guts.

But when you get specific about what you want, I can do it. I can tell you what I'm eating right now, as I peck this message out to you in bits and bats: a probably-terrible-for-me ready meal of lamb discs and carrot batons, swimming in a watery gravy.

It tastes about half as good as brown rice and broccoli sounds, but somewhere along the way to where I am now I forgot how to cook. Or maybe I never really learned? As a teenager I subsisted on floury cheese sauce made in the microwave, over pasta that I always managed to boil to death. University was a mess of those death noodles you mentioned, with the occasional slice of toast in between.

Though sometimes I do entertain ideas of more. Of fancy restaurants or hearty home-cooked meals; salads with dressings and sauces made from scratch. Pies with real crusts, gleaming and crisp. Cakes with sweet icing swirls and meat so tender it dissolves in the mouth…

Yeah, I dream about amazing food more than I actually eat it.

As for the book, and the bath:

Little Children, by Tom Perrotta.

And it was so good, I read until the water was flat cold. It had the glossy, enthralling sheen to it that American sadness often seems to have—as opposed to British sadness, which is always so droopy by comparison. We set a cow on fire in a field and go in lifts that stink of piss. Everything is damp and dark and just misses okay by a pathetic margin.

Affairs are conducted in gloomy silence at the seaside.

Thunder never rolls in the distance. There are never any haunting train sounds or bright blue pools or laundry rooms. Nobody finds any poetry.

Not even in our books.

The one I'm starting tonight is already grim and waterlogged. There's masturbation in it, but the masturbation is a terse, depressing, single-sentence affair. Like any further reflection on it would bring the tone of the book down, or give proceedings a slightly exciting air.

Nothing can be slightly exciting here.

Not even my messages to you, apparently, because now I'm fighting with myself again about whether I should have sent those last few lines. I've said a sexual word in front of you, in the middle of our texts about broccoli and being drunk and suffering through depression.

Though I suppose you did say that thing about Chat Roulette, first.

Can I be forgiven for masturbation, when you featured flapping dicks before I did?

8.28am

I wouldn't worry about scandalizing me with casual mentions of dreary literary masturbation. Sex has always been easy for me to talk about. It's probably the one genuine thing about me. In my old life I was all about artifice and airs, except when it came to sex.

But you seem shy about it, so I won't say much more than that. We've got kind of a pure thing going on here, and I promise I'm not secretly getting off on all this. Typing with one hand, as it were. It's not like that. I'm a gentleman pervert.

Plus, to be honest, sex is pretty far from my mind these days. Eroticism's in short supply around here, what with the catatonic toddler and my impending alcoholism.

Anyhow, I was thinking. Let's play a game, stranger. Truth or Dare, minus the dare part. We get to ask each other questions, and the other person has to answer them completely truthfully. We each get one pass. Deal?

Here's one for you: How long has it been since you left your apartment, really? I know you know. How could you not?

9.52am

Is it okay to admit that I liked you calling yourself a gentleman pervert?

Or tell you that I'm not that shy?

I just need to know where the line is, in case I'm the one being ungentlemanly.

And I like the idea of truth or dare. It's good and specific. It makes me feel like I'm not really answering at all, while answering pretty dreaded questions. I mean, I don't even think I've told myself when I really last left, never mind you.

It took me an hour to work out when it actually was. An hour of pretending I had to clean the bathroom instead of coming up with the number right now. I polished the mirror over the medicine cabinet and scrubbed the bath to a high gloss before I finally gave in and counted.

And now I think I have it: seven months ago I had to grab a parcel that someone had left outside my apartment door. Though does that technically count if it was just in the hallway? It felt like it counted. I had to reach outside while lying down, and when I was done my body was slick with sweat and sort of limp like an old dishrag.

Now here's my question for you:

Who did you think I was?

9.46pm

First off, apologies. I suggest a game, and then I disappear all day. To be honest…

To be honest, I just don't fucking know if I'm ready for that one. I tried wording my reply, even started tapping the words out now and then, between errands and chores, but it never looked right. The letters weren't coming together how I needed them to. The words were all wrong on my screen, like they weren't real words at all, and so I deleted them, again and again.

I feel like an ass, passing on the very first question of a game I started, but games should be fun, I decided. We've built a nice little playground here so far, and I don't want to be the cat that shits in the sandbox.

I'll tell you sometime, promise. But not tonight.

Ask me another?

10.02pm

I'm going to start out this letter-message with a plea: don't feel like an ass!

If you want to go lighter, we can go lighter.

How about this, then: top five films.

No shame over cheesiness is allowed, all answers are valid, films that you just can't stop watching if they come on the telly are completely permissible.

I will be over here, compiling my own list with so much agonising care you'd think I was a Professor of Doing Top Fives of Things.

11.45pm

Now we're talking, Professor Stranger.

Top five, though? That's tough. I've got a notepad balanced here on my thigh, with six million titles scribbled down and crossed out and starred and underlined. Ultimately I decided I better approach this challenge from the desert island angle, like these are the only five movies I get to watch for the rest of my life, not necessarily the five best or most important movies ever made.

I'd want a mix. Something that leaves me bawling like a little bitch. Something that makes me laugh until I nearly pee—maybe two of those. Something from my childhood. Something that makes me think deep thoughts…

So here we go.

Fuck, this feels like such a monumental proclamation.

Okay, I think mine are: The Green Mile. The Jerk. Being John Malkovich. National Lampoon's Christmas Vacation (for both nostalgia and seasonality, because the holidays get lonely on a desert island). And guilty pleasure admission, Aladdin. Don't tell the cool kids. I know ALL the words to ALL the songs. In my defense, I was nine when it came out.

How about you? Top five movies, plus the top five TV show box sets you'd pack to bring to your lonely island. Go.

WEDNESDAY

12.02am

I was just on the verge of drifting off when your messages pinged through, one after the other. But only because I assumed you'd gone to sleep too. As soon as I heard the evidence that you hadn't I was wide awake again, devouring everything you had to say.

Those are excellent choices.

And by excellent I mean they are both cool enough, and yet not so cool that I feel I have to lie about my own choices. If you had been one of those guys who lists obscure silent movies in French that were lost during the war, or macho films about gangsters probably played by Al Pacino, I might have pretended I loved stuff directed by Jean Luc Goddard.

Even though I honestly have no idea who he is.

He's just the fanciest director I could think of.

But now I can be totally, one hundred percent honest. Here is my list, in all of its weird glory: Splash, Fargo, The Truth About Cats and Dogs, The Silence of the Lambs, Candyman.

Splash because I was so obsessed as a kid I once secretly made myself a tail, Fargo because catching criminals while my cuddly bald husband waited at home just seemed like the best kind of life to me, The Silence of the Lambs because of my lovely Clarice, my Clarice god I wanted to be Clarice so bad. The Truth About Cats and Dogs because it's a meeting of minds not beautiful faces. And Candyman, because it's a horror movie.

But also because it's a romance.

Now, box sets.

I want to say Blackadder, but there are so few episodes. And it's the same for American Gothic, even though I loved that show unreasonably. Dungeons and Dragons would have to go in, for old times' sake.

But then I'm still so short on episodes.

Star Trek: The Next Generation would probably help out there. Does that get me to five? No, I need one more. Another long one, a juicier one. Maybe Dexter?

Yeah, Dexter.

Okay, your turn. And don't skimp on the reasons!

1.40am

Nope, my days of pretending to like clever, obscure shit are over. The only people that crap ever impresses are insecure assholes, and I'm the only insecure asshole I've got room for in my life at this point. Jean Luc Goddard can suck it.

(Though I did like Weekend, legitimately. You should check it out. That plus Silence of the Lambs and you've got a cannibalism double feature!)

I hadn't considered the quantity versus quality conundrum… Would I rather watch endless episodes of something kinda entertaining, or just a few episodes that are all genius? Shit.

Let's just plunge in. Your scary movie picks are making me want all the old Tales from the Crypts. We had HBO for a couple years when I was little, and I remember staying up late, waiting for that show like it was a religion. No clue if they'd be any good as a grown-up, but I'd be willing to find out.

It's probably a girl show, but I fucking love me some Six Feet Under. That's just good TV. If our islands are adjacent, we could trade our Michael C. Hall stashes back and forth via a complex coconut raft and tether system.

For some reason, I think bringing every episode of The Bachelor or Survivor would be smart. I've never seen a single minute of either, but it seems like there's a lot of episodes per season and a lot of seasons, so there's quantity, plus I think The Bachelor would curb any torturous yearnings for civilization I might be tempted to suffer. Or I would become completely obsessed and overly emotionally involved. Either way, let's throw one of those in the mix.

Duck Tales. If you didn't grow up with Duck Tales, you basically had no childhood worth mentioning.

I think I need another quality collection to balance out the irony and nostalgia…something funny but well-written.

Oh shit, back up! I need to swap out Duck Tales and bring The Simpsons instead. Gazillions of episodes, even if I'd probably only ever fire up seasons two through eight. SNL is also a temptation for sheer volume, but I think I've made the right choice here.

And since that covers the funny factor, my final pick would be The X-Files. That one's nostalgia, too, but also good writing, for the most part.

Now you—top five pop songs. The ones you never, ever switch the channel on when they come on the radio. Cheesier the better.

2.22am

I'm so glad I asked you not to skimp on reasons. Your reasons are so good. Like getting overly emotionally involved in The Bachelor, which I can completely see happening to me too. I would probably intend to stay aloof and ironic about it. But then the bachelor would choose Jessie over Susie and it would be bedlam.

Oh and yes yes yes a thousand times yes to Six Feet Under. I almost said that, but then wondered if it would make me seem obsessed with Hall. Even though I swear to god I barely noticed him when I first watched that show. And any feelings I have about Dexter are purely to do with him being essentially Batman.

If we were honest about what Batman does.

As for the rest if your choices: I would definitely need you to create the pulley system. I need Simpsons and X-Files and even Tales from the Crypt, even though I distinctly remember seeing an episode as a kid and not sleeping for the rest of my life.

Now: pop songs.

1. The Safety Dance by Men Without Hats. Both because it's a lighthearted pop song and also because it's probably what will play to herald the coming of our doom at the hands of a goblin army.

2. What Is Love by Haddaway. Probably for the same reason? I can definitely see Satan riding in on his chariot to this tune.

3. Push the Button by The Sugababes. Surely this must be a humiliating enough choice? They spell sugar wrong in their name. And yet I feel that this song is everything good about music.

4. I'm Like a Bird by Nelly Furtado. I think this might actually be an excellent choice. The kind of choice that posh, cultured people would make to diversify their lists of joyless dirges. But I'm putting it here anyway because it's impossible to not.

5. Irreplaceable by Beyoncé. This has to go on the list, because not long ago I discovered to my total shock that it is the number

one played song on my iPod. By an insanely huge amount. Like so insanely huge I'm a little concerned I've been sleepwalking to the sound of it playing.

Hopefully that was cheesy enough for you.

Now hit me with your own cheese.

4.29am

Jesus fuck, why am I not asleep?

Because we're basically curating mix tapes, is why. I can agonize for days just over the song order in a mix, especially if there's a girl involved. And there is, of course, though we're making anti-mix-tapes, here, all cheese and no dignity. It's kind of a relief.

Okay, here goes.

1. Say, Say, Say. You know, that duet between Michael Jackson and Paul McCartney, and it had an amazing video where they're snake-oil salesmen traveling around in a Conestoga wagon in the Old West or something? It's probably not either of their best work, but I fucking love it. I bet it makes it onto 90+ percent of my road trip mixes.

2. Since U Been Gone, by Kelly Clarkson. I love bitter-ass break-up songs, and that one is solid gold.

3. Cry Me a River, by Justin Timberlake. Same reason.

4. Nothing's Gonna Stop Us Now, by Starship. Theme to the movie Mannequin? I bet my mom played that single eight thousand times when I was little. It's seared onto my brain like grill marks. If I ever find out that by freak coincidence we live in the same village, I'm going to celebrate by drugging you and rolling you in a wheelbarrow to the nearest karaoke bar and forcing you to perform it with me.

5. It's All Coming Back to Me Now, by Meatloaf. I don't know why, but I can't hear that song and not cry. Like, full-on sobbing if I'm alone, or feigned-allergy sniffles if there are witnesses. Don't tell anyone.

Since we're on the topic of cheesiness, can I just say thank you for this? I've got so much shit going on, but for the twenty minutes it took me to pick those songs, I was a teenager again. Not to say that I want to forget about the boy, necessarily, but it was kinda miraculous that I managed to, just now, with you. So thanks for that.

Now, for the next top five... How about top five villains of all time, in any sort of media?

One of mine is definitely Murdoch from MacGyver. He made me want to grow up to be an assassin.

Gus from Breaking Bad was amazing.

Miss Hannigan from the 1982 movie version of Annie, because I have a sort of quasi-Oedipal crush on Carol Burnett, who reminds me of my mom a little. Don't read too much into that. Plus Burnett made alcoholism look like way more fun than it actually is in that movie.

Hans Gruber from Die Hard. Clearly I love my villains cool and calculating and smarter than the hero.

And finally…damn, let's think…

Oh, I know! Dark Helmet, from Space Balls. I don't think that one needs any justification.

Now you, stranger.

3.23pm

Sorry for taking so long to reply. Though I suppose it hasn't been that long, really. It just feels like a long time, when I'm busy making myself do necessary morning things instead of immediately pouncing on your 4am messages. If my mind had its way, I think I'd forgo eating breakfast and taking a shower, just to get back to this more quickly.

But I made myself be good. I got up at eleven and ate some cereal and washed up and got dressed and answered emails, before finally giving in.

And you can say thank you. As long as I can thank you.

I had no idea that sharing lists of things you love could be so soothing—both to compile, and to read from someone else. It makes me think about things I haven't thought of for years. Like it's blowing away cobwebs I didn't realise had gathered in my mind. And it gives me a picture of you I doubt a thousand emotional back and forths could have revealed.

Not that I think I know you, though, because you told me you like Nothing's Gonna Stop Us Now. Just that I feel I know you a little better—and in a different way to the way I might have known you if you told me you were happy or sad.

Does that make sense?

I hope so.

Because now I'm going to move right on into my villains.

Hans Gruber obviously. I don't even care if you think I'm copying you!

It has to be. The universe demands it.

Hannibal Lecter.

Partly because he is amazing, but also because of that line he says to Clarice. You know the one about the mirror? I think about that a lot. About someone being so evil and yet revering goodness so completely.

Only in the movies, I guess.

But then, isn't that why we love them?

So we can love the villains we would hate in real life?

My other three are Severen from Near Dark, Jareth from Labyrinth, and Agent Smith from The Matrix.

But only because their evil is on the other side of the safety glass that is my TV.

And my next question is: top five places you would go, if you could.

10.17pm

The five places I'd go if I could… I've been mulling it over all evening, while I got the boy fed and down for the night and poured myself a drink and then a second, and I have to say, I'm dying to know your answers to this one. It almost feels pornographic, the thought of hearing where an agoraphobe fantasizes about traveling to.

Maybe that's the whiskey texting, but I dunno. It strikes me as a grotesquely intimate thing to discover about you.

My immediate reaction when you asked was to type "home," meaning Albuquerque. But when I think about it, I don't feel what I'd expected. I don't feel achy with homesickness, dying to get back there. The thing is, I don't feel like I know who I am anymore, and going back there… I think it'd be really confusing and uncomfortable.

When I left, I thought I was a hip, successful, relevant member of a social tribe. Now I'm here, and I'm a lonely, half-competent-at-best, quite possibly alcoholic single father. There's not a lot of overlap to those identities.

I feel like I know myself better now, but I like myself less. Or rather, I want to be my own self less. I don't know how to translate my new self within the context of my old life. So no, Albuquerque's not making the list.

So let's just have fun with it, shall we?

First off, Patagonia, because it looks fucking gorgeous.

Morocco, just to wander around massive outdoor markets buying dried fruits I can't identify and likely getting pickpocketed by trained monkeys.

Somewhere northern enough to see the Northern Lights. Maybe get drunk enough to weep with wonder while sitting on the banks of an Icelandic river or something.

New Orleans. I've never been, and that seems like my loss. It looks so sexy and strange and nasty and alive.

And finally, Paris. Personally, I don't have any particular affection for the French, but my mom always wanted to go there. She bought way deep into the romance of the idea of Paris, so I'd go and do all the things I bet she'd have liked. Every touristy, flouncy, beret-capped Parisian thing there is to be done. And I'd buy a dozen girly postcards to bring home, and I'd pin them up around my house and pretend she sent them to me and imagine her wandering around all those places with a baguette under her arm.

Now you. Relieve me of this smothering curiosity, already.

THURSDAY

6.43am

I can't believe I slept through your messages pinging. Usually I can't sleep through anything, even if anything is nothing at all. But I woke up refreshed—more than I've been in a while. So I'm going to reward myself by answering right away:

I never thought of it that way. About that question revealing even more about me, because I never go anywhere. But now I'm wondering if that's why I didn't answer, before sending you the question. Like there's a block in my mind, even when we're just talking fantasy destinations. Even pretend plane journeys make me panic, apparently.

Either that, or I'm embarrassed.

You said such sophisticated, grown-up places.

And all I want to do is slip through the back of a wardrobe and into Narnia. Or climb a faraway tree and find revolving worlds up there. Or wash up in Oz in the middle of the desert that turns you to stone. Or ask the goblin king to take me away to the labyrinth right now.

Those are the places I would go if I could. Other worlds, vast and terrible and beautiful and weird. Places where magic is real, because oh I get so tired of all this relentless mundanity.

Not even just relentless, really—violent mundanity.

The kind that asserts itself aggressively, just as you think everything is going to be amazing. You buy that perfect dress and then catch yourself in a shop window, looking dull and lumpy and grey. The success you had turns into a grind; the beautiful flat you bought becomes a prison.

The ceiling leaks. The neighbours hate you.

Whatever future you imagined is now a long-distant memory.

I'd brave dragons in Earthsea to be away from all of that.

Is that so crazy? I think it might be crazy.

Let's talk about something less crazy, like books.

Top five books.

8.27am

Don't be embarrassed. Hell, I'm kind of embarrassed now, since you asked where I'd go if I could go anywhere and I wasn't creative enough to think of made-up places.

If I had occasion to kidnap you, I'd take you places that make Earth seem magical. Like lava tube caves, or to the desert at sunset, or to that Icelandic lakeside under the Northern Lights…as long as you're prepared to deal with my drunken weeping.

I can't take you to Narnia, but there's places here that are still pretty amazing. Bonus: you're less likely to get eaten or turned to stone here in the real world.

I'm further embarrassed to tell you about my favorite books, because you clearly know what you're talking about, and for the past decade or more I've typically read whatever's popular—but not TOO popular, mind, because hipster cred. Basically, whatever book I thought might convince an interesting woman to sleep with me, should she spot me holding it in a coffee shop.

But that doesn't say anything about me, does it? Apart perhaps from my prurient applications of conspicuous literacy. It doesn't tell you anything of substance, to be sure, nothing worth knowing about me, and I think that's what you're after.

So let's see…what books would I actually want with me on that desert island, where there are no witnesses?

Let's just get this out there right off the bat—my favorite book is probably Jurassic Park. I'm not saying it's the best book ever written, but it's the one I've read more than any other, discounting the books from my childhood. (I read Hatchet about a hundred times, and White Fang maybe twice that.)

To make matters worse, let's stick another Crichton on the list—Andromeda Strain.

Okay, I think I need to muster some variety, here. Let's see, number three… Oh, I've liked a lot of Chuck Palahniuk's books. Especially Choke. There might be some outdated hipster posing mixed in there, but I do genuinely like his storytelling.

Number four. How about Life of Pi? I picked that up in a Barnes and Noble when I was about twenty-five, thinking I'd peek at the first page, and then wound up reading the entire thing without ever leaving the store. That'd never happened to me before and hasn't since, but I do hope it happens again someday. I drank about five coffees over the course of the afternoon and, unable to put it down, read some of the book while peeing in the store bathroom. For that reason, ethics compelled me to purchase the copy.

And number five, I'm thinking maybe something nostalgic. Let's go with Holes. I fucking LOVED Holes. I'll totally be giving that to the boy when he's old enough.

Wait a second, that's so lame—I don't have a single book written by a woman. Maybe you could recommend me some, based on my ridiculous short list. My nights are long, so I promise I'll read each and every one you prescribe.

But not before you tell me what books a certain booklover loves best.

10.42am

You make me want to be kidnapped so badly, right here and right now as I sit in my pyjamas just finishing up my breakfast. All those places you said—I could almost believe that here isn't so violently mundane after all. When you describe our world, it sounds like dragons are just around the corner and magic is so close I could breathe it in.

I appreciate that. And all your books.

I've never been the sort to judge something people read for enjoyment. What better motive is there for reading then to fall into the familiar? To have fun, far away from whatever we have to deal with here?

In my opinion, Jurassic Park fits that bill perfectly. I love that it's just a little more twisted than the movie. That Hammond isn't the cosy-old-misguided-but-sweet-grandpops type. And even though Crichton himself is a bit of a tool, I go out of my mind for all that goofy pseudoscience stuff.

He's got a way with info and detail. I'll give him that.

Anyway, my fave books…

I'll see you a Crichton and raise you a King. The Talisman, most probably. Just because it's that disappearing-into-other-worlds thing again.

Earthsea, by Ursula Le Guin. If you need a woman to read, she's your gal. Especially Tehanu, because it's beautiful and amazing.

Another woman: Octavia Butler. Kindred. God, you can almost taste and feel everything she writes about. It's raw and good and science fiction about things no one else writes science fiction about.

I suppose I should have something less fantastical on my list so:

Notes on a Scandal, by Zoe Heller.

It's almost a memoir, the main character is so real. Like you can't believe she doesn't exist. And you hate her you hate her you hate while aching inside over her loneliness.

Finally, something from my childhood too. Monster, by Christopher Pike.

Gory and viscous, but with this great melancholy core.

And with that, I am out of lists.

How about this: last meal on earth?

FRIDAY

12.39am

Sorry about the radio silence, stranger.

The boy's grandmother came over to watch him so I could deal with some legal crap to do with paternity and the boy's citizenship options and on and on. The only upside is that I can now casually toss out the phrase "met with my solicitor today" and feel a little British about it.

When I got back, the boy's aunt was here—his mom's sister. I've only met her once before, so as much as I wanted to pull out my phone and check all those precious messages I'd felt buzzing against my butt way back when I was leaving this morning, etiquette compelled me to be a half-decent host.

There was a lot to talk about. Heavy shit. Once they left and the boy was in bed, I had to just sit by the window and have a drink and turn it all around in my head, get it filed away and set aside before I finally read your texts.

Last meal on earth, you say? A classic conundrum.

I love food. I'm a good cook. I have about ten things I can cook really well, and I think that's all you need.

If my mom was still here, I'd want her to cook my last meal, but failing that I'd do it myself. (Not because I'm amazing or anything, just because I'll miss cooking once I'm dead.)

I'd pick out every ingredient and probably marinate something overnight. Steak, likely. Really good steak, grilled rare. Asparagus if it's in season. Corn on the cob. Garlic potatoes with loads of butter. I'd invite you to join me, but I wouldn't be upset if you couldn't come. I'd understand.

Now here's your next question: What question do you most wish I'd ask you? And what would your answer be?

1.33am

I just knew you'd be a good cook. I could sense it. Though I had no idea it would torture me so much to hear it. Here I am at one in the morning, bleary-eyed from the doze I'd just drifted into, and instead of going right back to sleep I'm drooling over your food.

Oh, I can almost taste the butter and garlic on the potatoes. I can nearly hear the sizzle of the meat. Maybe I can even see you doing it—though of course most of your features are blurred out, like an innocent passerby on a crime-prevention programme.

Also I'm now furious at my fridge for only containing microwave meals.

Tomorrow, I swear I'm going to order better food.

Food from a fancy restaurant.

And then when I eat, I'll pretend you made it.

Even though you're a sly one, to ask me such a crafty question. Now I will have to reveal double about myself—once in asking, and again in answering. Two for the price of one, as it were. Oh yeah, don't think I didn't notice! But as I'm still busy dining on your steak in my head, I will answer. And I'll even give you a humiliating slice of my inner life, with it:

I would want you to ask me how my day was, like I live in a cheesy sitcom set in the suburbs. You put your coat on a hook and sit down at a huge dining table in an enormous kitchen, and then I tell you all about the cheese and pickle sandwich I had, and the sheets I ordered from Dunhelm, and the article I read online.

But most importantly, I would tell you about the window.

I opened the living room window for the first time in years, and stuck my hand out so I could feel the rain. It was warm, much warmer than I remember it being, and the smell of the air sung inside my body.

Now you go. You tell me what you would want me to ask, and how you would answer.

5.35am

I should really be asleep. The boy wakes up by seven most days, and I only got three hours tonight before his dreams woke him and he needed me.

Well, I say "needed me." I'm not sure if I really help him much. I just sort of squeeze him and rock us back and forth on his bed until he stops moaning, and when he falls silent but is still breathing fast, I sing to him. Tonight I sang

Thunder Road, which is a ridiculous song to sing to a child who's having night terrors, but I don't think it made anything worse, so, hey. Parenting.

I'm rambling here, because to be completely honest, your last text left me a little flustered. Not, like, frustrated. Like, weirdly sweaty and warm in the face.

Warm all over.

Warm from the way you describe imagining what I cook.

Warm to think maybe you'll order something fancy someday and think of me while you eat it.

Warm because you made me laugh, with that throwaway comment about the blurry-faced passerby. I haven't laughed in so long. I mean, I laugh for the boy's benefit when we're watching TV, a pantomime sort of laugh. But you made me laugh for real.

Did the rain on your hand feel as good as that laugh did? I hope so.

That made me warm as well, you talking about the rain and the air. You have a way of making the mundane sound… sensual. I want to backtrack and say not in a sexual way, but that's not strictly true. It's pretty fucking erotic.

I'm deliriously tired, and all my social filters have gone to bed, so there you are.

Can I join your fantasy and make it all old-timey? As you're telling me about your day, can I toss my fedora smartly on the coatrack, then stride to the hutch where I keep my classy crystal decanter of Scotch and pour myself a glass?

Here's where the fantasy falls apart, though, because in this black-and-white world I'd probably wear trouser socks, just like you'd wear pantyhose with seams up the calves. But here in reality I'd most likely plop down sideways on the chair next to yours and wedge my bare feet under your nearest thigh, and flex my achy toes, and one of them would probably pop, and that's not very sexy, but reality rarely is.

I'd make it up to you by asking what you want for dinner, and hopefully it would be one of the ten things I'm really good at. Maybe Moroccan lamb stew, if it's cold and dreary out.

Maybe I put the slow cooker on before I left that morning so you could smell it simmering all afternoon. I wonder if you'd sneak tastes or make yourself wait? That'd tell me so much about you.

I'd ask you all about the sheets, what thread count and what color, and what sort of cheese you used in the sandwich, and did you toast the bread, and was the article any good?

Is it completely patronizing to say that I'm proud of you for opening the window?

Is it creepy to say I got especially warm at how you said it sung inside your body?

Is it weird to say that now I feel as though I haven't really lived, having never kissed a woman and tasted cheese and pickle on her lips?

None of these count as my question, by the way. Rhetorical and all. My real question this round is, have you ever been in love?

As for your question…

I'd want you to ask me my name.

And I'd tell you it's Malcolm.

6.07am

Oh god, what a thing to wake up to.

I don't know where to begin.

Or I do know where to begin.

I'm just afraid of all the things I want to begin with.

It's that feeling again of am I saying too much? Or maybe going too far?

But I just have to tell you that you make toe popping sound really…something that I'm too embarrassed to label sexy. For a second I could almost feel them under my bare thigh, cold and yet somehow warming at the same time. Intimate, I think the word is, though to be honest I have no real idea at all.

I've never been close enough with anyone to just have little habits like that.

To maybe sneak a taste of their delicious stew—because I totally would. I could never wait for something like that, for something made with care for me by another person, for something that simmers and comes out of a slow cooker and sounds like sheer bliss.

My mouth is flooding just thinking about it.

My mouth is flooding just thinking about your other questions, oh your questions, oh you've no idea what a luxury questions are to me. They make me want to whisper in your ear instead of telling you across a table. About the cheese, which was soft and sweet, and the sheets that have buttons on them and fold so crisp and clean, and the article…

It was all about evidence that we aren't alone in the universe.

And no no no it's never patronising. No, it's never creepy.

It's the opposite, whatever the opposite of patronising and creepy is.

It sings inside my body too.

Makes me want to ask what you would taste like, if I were to taste you.

God. God. I have to…just stop there.

6.25am

Damn, I forgot to respond to your question.

Though I think you know the answer anyway.

No, I've never been in love.

Have you, Malcolm?

10.59am

I got a legit shiver, when I first read your reply. A shiver I just had to sit inside all morning, waiting for a chance to sit down and respond properly.

I've long known that hearing my name in certain breathy, vigorous contexts is like sex kryptonite for me, but I never would have guessed that reading it in a text could do that.

TMI? It's, like, lunchtime, so I can't blame it on delirium or booze. Oh well. What's sent is sent.

For a second, I thought how sad it is that you've never been in love. But then I thought harder about it, and in a way maybe it's not. It means you still get to feel that for the first time.

Actually, after I asked you that question, I regretted it. I thought, what if she asks me the same? Because I'm not very proud of my answer, to be honest.

In short, I've been in love. I've been in love so many times I'm beginning to wonder, have I actually ever been in love?

I fall in love easily. I'm quick to toss those three little words around, like they're singles instead of fifties. Or the old me was. He was way better at falling in love than actually maintaining a relationship, though.

In hindsight, I had a pattern: see a girl, interact with her briefly, then construct an elaborate, baseless, two-dimensional concept in my head of who she is and how dating her would so perfectly accessorize and complete my life.

Fast forward. By the three, four, five-month mark, everyone's resentful and disappointed. Inevitably. The poor woman's fallen short of my ill-informed and unrealistic expectations about who she is, and often vice versa, because I put up plenty of fronts of my own.

The breakups always took weeks, too. These grinding emotional autopsies before the wretched, long-suffering relationship could finally be declared dead.

My romantic history is basically that Gotye song on repeat for four hours. Super fraught and beautifully tortured at first, then by the fifteenth time you're like ENOUGH WITH THE FUCKING XYLOPHONE.

I'm totally to blame. I wasn't equipped to date actual human beings. I fell for a woman's quirky dress sense or her tattoos or her art, one thing or another, then once the novelty wore off I'd lose interest. I'm cringing even typing this, but I feel compelled to be honest with you.

It sounds shallow. It probably was a little shallow, but more than that, I think I just felt empty. I was always searching for that perfect, unique, fascinating woman to stitch myself to, so I could quit feeling like half a human.

That's too much to ask of someone. To complete you.

I wasn't prepared for any of my exes to be actual people with their own feelings and faults. I was only worried about what being with them said about me. I often wound up with people just like me. Big on facades, but lost and echoing inside.

So while I've said "I love you" a dozen times and meant it, a part of me wonders, do I really even know what that feels like?

There's got to be more than whatever I felt, because I was able to walk away from it again and again.

But something about you, about this, gives me hope. That suddenly I have a crush on someone based on nothing more than her words. Her thoughts. Her fears and dreams and cheese sandwiches.

No artifice, only substance. Sort of odd, mysterious, charming and sometimes ridiculous substance, but I like that. I can dig my fingers into it. It's strange and squishy with funny lumps, but it feels good. So fucking good and real after swiping at holograms for all these years.

I don't even know your age or your hair color or the sound of your voice or your name, but I like you. That gives me hope. Hope that maybe someday I'll quit falling in love and simply love. I've always chased the noun, when maybe I should have been trying to master the verb.

I can't believe I'm even typing all this to you. So soon. We've been chatting for what, four or five days?

I don't even care if you're secretly an old married guy or a cruel computer algorithm or a hyperintelligent cat.

I don't care that you can't leave the house and I'm in no position to attempt a relationship right now.

Whatever this is, it's exactly what I want. I want your words. Unpredictable, inexplicable, kind, addictive words coming at me out of nowhere on a tiny screen. Lighting up my face and pillow in a dark bedroom or compelling my fingers to keep tapping tapping tapping while I make lunch. (Cold chicken sandwiches; I've got a mayonnaise smear on my phone, rainbow-izing my pixels.)

Better get the boy fed. But here's my next question for you: what would you like for your birthday?

P.S. I love that you wouldn't wait. I love that you'd steal impatient tastes on the sly.

P.P.S. When you described your mouth flooding it did unspeakable things to me.

P.P.P.S. My mouth currently tastes like stale black coffee, but ask me again in twelve hours and I'll say bourbon. And I'll probably say some other things once that bourbon starts working that I won't with the sun still shining.

4.17pm

I don't care that it was lunchtime. I do care that I sex-kryptonited you. My whole body fizzed when I read that—and the weird thing is I don't even mind admitting it.

Probably because you admit things too. You say things like "crush" and "like" long before I do, and it eases open the heavy metal doors I usually put around any of my needier feelings. It makes them seem less needy and more reasonable.

Even after as little as five days.

Though I'll be honest: it staggered me when you said them. In my little dark den, time is often fluid and foggy. I think it's the fourth of June when it's really ten weeks last Tuesday. But this whole thing has made time even bendier. Suddenly decades are being squeezed into five minutes. It feels like I've known you forever.

I'm forgetting what it was like to not do this.

To not be glad for you and your realisation about love. To root for you to find that person who isn't just the idea of what you want. To imagine the unspeakable things.

Then think about doing them to you.

And the bourbon on your lips…

I went to sleep this afternoon thinking of the bourbon on your lips. Like syrupy sunlight, I imagine it tastes—because honestly I have no real idea. I've never had a single sip of the stuff, but oh I would drink a barrel of it down if it came to me from you.

In fact, that's what I would ask for, for my birthday.

A case of you.

What would you want, in return?

9.10pm

Greetings from the chair by the window. Socks off, feet on the sill, radiator ticking.

A case of me, huh? Was that a Joni Mitchell reference, stranger? If we kissed, would it taste so bitter and so sweet?

Hopefully not too bitter. Sweet with a sting, because, as promised, I'm drinking bourbon now that I'm off-duty, relatively speaking.

Not a big dose, just a single on ice. It's clinking softly in this quiet room, the glass glinting in the light of the reading lamp.

Rain's streaking and pattering at the window, and while this time last week that fact would have depressed me, tonight it's…I'm not sure. Atmospheric? That's a ten-dollar word, but it's still not quite right. There ought to be an adjective for when something's at once melancholy and seductive. Perhaps the French have one.

It feels like longing, distilled.

What would I want in return, you ask? Let's stick with Ms. Mitchell.

For my birthday, I want you here, or me there. I want the summer, because my birthday's in late June. I want us on a couch, and the windows open, and the breeze dry and cooling as the sun drops. Thanks to you, I want the first time we kiss to have Car on a Hill be playing, because that song is sexy as fuck. Then Help Me, because goddamn.

You'd taste the bourbon, and what would I taste, I wonder? Do you drink wine? Do you drink at all? Would I taste mint from your toothpaste or gum, or some lingering salty tang from whatever it is I made us for dinner? Or would I just taste you?

Would it be slow as molasses, or fast and frantic and grasping, like the thrashing of a drowning man? I can't even guess, and that makes me want to imagine it all the more.

Are you there, stranger? Reading every line as it makes your phone shiver or ping?

Tell me what you imagine.

9.53pm

I love that you know the song.

That you know I want sting when I say bitter.

And that you described all of that to me. Oh, your descriptions are blissful. I can almost see that glinting, can almost hear the sound of ice against glass. Every word you just said sunk me deeper into that glowing light and the heat of some summer we're not actually in. Into those kisses, heavy with alcohol and sweet with cinnamon—because that's what I taste like.

Always cinnamon, from the sugar on cookies or the centres of sweets.

And I would be frantic, definitely frantic. There is no way I could be slow with something like kissing. Not after so long imagining what it would be like. Not when I've seen it a thousand ways through the TV screen but never actually felt it. Just hearing you suggest it is enough to make me feel half starved—greedy for something slick and soft against my lips.

For hands, too, would there be hands?

I want there to be hands.

In my hair, on my back, on me all over.

You'd feel me shiver if you did. Hell, if you strain hard I'm sure you could feel me through your phone. My teeth are practically chattering; there are goose bumps all over my arms. Like I'm afraid almost—though maybe I am? It feels like terror, this terrible charge running through me. It makes me want to burst out of my own skin.

And once I had, I would run to you.

Tell me that you would run to me too.

10.26pm

I could run to you. Our bodies could meet with a force that borders on violence, charged with ferocious desperation.

Or I could be still as a rock, watch you running. Watch you growing closer, closer, features coming into focus, and brace myself like I was standing before a rushing wave, and let you crash over me, drown in all that need and curiosity.

Or I could come up behind you in a quiet room or a crowded train station or a damp and lonely park. Curl a palm around your shoulder and turn you, slowly. Study the surprise and recognition in your eyes for a long breath before I brought my mouth down on yours.

What color are those eyes? Don't tell me brown, blue, green, hazel. Be specific. Tell me maple syrup, tell me the sky in winter, sea glass, bay leaf.

And yes, there would be hands. Before our lips ever meet, there are hands.

Mine are homely, my fingertips dry and hard as horn from playing the guitar.

One is on your throat, thumb on your jugular so I can feel your pulse, fierce and frantic. The other thumb is at your temple, fingers in your hair, palm covering your ear so it rushes like the ocean.

What does that hair feel like?

And your hands. Tell me about them, stranger. Tell me what they feel like and where they are on me. Where they are and where they don't yet dare to go.

10.43pm

The train station, yes, I want the train station. Your mouth on mine before we've even had a chance to be awkward with each other. No stuttered hellos and shaking of sweaty hands. No remarks about the traffic getting there or the delays on platform three. Just your mouth, and then that warm pressure. Those hands where you said they would go.

I've often imagined someone touching me like that. Cradling my head, my throat, holding me in place for a kiss. Somehow I always thought the reality would be his hands held loosely at his sides. That he wouldn't have enough imagination to do anything more, unless the more was groping my breasts or tugging off my underwear.

I'm under no illusions about real life.

And yet you make me believe in something so much sweeter.

You make me spend ages coming up with just the right colour of my eyes—something pretty, but also something that isn't lies. They are smooth stones at the bottom of the ocean, dull at first glance, I think, but hinting at a hidden blue light. And when I'm done with thinking this up, I turn to my hands, as soft and plump as sleeping birds.

They look new, my hands. As if I've never done a thing with them.

I suppose I haven't. I've never slid my fingers over the hard slant of a man's shoulder blade, searching for all the grooves and jutting parts that I so long to feel. I don't know what it's like to find the parts of his body that make him gasp and arch.

But I know where they are.

I think about where they are on you.

I would be thinking about them as you kissed me, on that platform.

Tell me more about kissing me on the platform.

11.19pm

I'd start softly, just a glancing of my lips, the tiniest bump of the tips of our noses, the mingling of shallow exhalations, the rough brush of my chin against yours. I'm habitually overdue for a shave, so while the touch is gentle, my jaw won't be. I hope that's all right.

I'd want to kiss you so softly that it's like a whisper in the crowd. Make you focus until the bustle of the platform fades to nothing and you can hear my breathing and the parting of our lips. So quiet I can hear the pulse that's thumping against my hand.

Now you tell me what comes next. If this is your first kiss, let's make it everything you've been wanting. Worthy of a movie.

It seems there's so much you've never experienced. I won't make a fetish of it, but I won't lie—I want to be the one to bring those things to you.

You say your hands are like birds. Have you heard of bowerbirds? I saw a documentary about them when I first moved here. They live in Papua New Guinea, and the males build these elaborate nests to impress the females. They stack and pile and ornament them with bright, ripe berries and shiny beetle shells and flowers and stones and all sorts of things.

That's what I'd want to do. Lay everything out before you, every sensation and sound and smell and sight and taste that comes with sex, sweet and dark and filthy alike, and watch you inspect and explore every one. Watch you unwrap each new thing like a candy and slip it past your lips, hover it under your nose, hold it to your ear or cup it in your hands.

Now you tell me, how do you want to be kissed?

11.50pm

Ohhhh yes that all sounds so good. The way you want to touch me. The things you want to offer me. But please don't be afraid of making it a fetish, if the fetish makes me feel like this.

All new and open and ready, just waiting for you to go farther.

Because that's what I want.

Farther.

More.

Faster.

Filthier.

I want your kisses somewhere other than my lips, every single one of them rough with that stubble, burning with that stubble. Turn the skin of my throat red with it, and don't you dare stop there. Every inch of my body is as pale as milk—it all needs marking. It needs you to score great grooves into the curves and planes, until I'm covered.

Until I'm gasping.

Because I know I would be. I run rough things over my throat, the slope of my breasts, my stomach, just thinking if that's how it would feel. And when I think I have it right, the air rushes out of me. Sounds push past my lips—ones that I've never let out before. Usually I put my fist in my mouth. I cover my face with a pillow.

But somehow I think that would be the wrong move with you.

I think you would want to hear me.

Oh god, I hope you would want to hear me.

SATURDAY

3.50am

Fucking hell.

In my head, I composed my next reply. It read, "I'm sorry, I can't do this. It feels so good, but I can't. I'm sorry. You're wonderful, but goodbye, stranger."

I assembled those words, a hundred variations of them, as I sat on the boy's bed, rocking him, rocking him, waiting for the moans to soften and go silent, for his shivers and shaking to still.

His terrors pulled me from your orbit as I was reveling in each new chime of my phone, jerked me out of the excitement and fantasy of you and into the next room and the sad and frantic reality I now call my daily life.

I thought, what the fuck am I doing? How can this possibly be okay? Where in my reality is there room for this hot, sweet madness?

And then, after I'd sung Past and Pending, and Soldier's Things, Sugar Mountain and half a dozen other songs, once I was so exhausted I wanted to sob, he fell back asleep.

I carried my restless body and my head full of apologies back to the living room and picked up my phone, and tried to make the words right. Typed them this way, that way, felt lost and deleted them. Had a drink. Scrolled back to the very beginning and read where we first started. Read on and on, and by the time I came to your latest texts, I knew I was wrong. That THIS isn't wrong, whatever this is.

That this is the only solace and escape and joy I have right now. The only good thing, just like I'd said. So good I doubt I deserve it, but how's a wretch lost in a desert going to pass up a drink of water, really?

I read your words, and I forgot the despair and the helplessness that eats me alive for hours a day here.

The things you wrote lit me up like a fucking bonfire. All over again, I felt things I haven't in so long. Desire and hunger and a strange, dark strain of confidence, even.

Confident because, yes, I can be all those things for you.

If I do have a fetish, it's to be exactly what a woman wants. That's always excited me more than anything else: to spoil someone, to ruin her for every other man who comes after, to be a slave and a whore and a zealot to her pleasure.

And yes, I want to hear you. More than you could ever know. Whatever your voice, whatever your accent, whatever words might fall from that mouth when I was finally done kissing it.

I want cautious and curious requests—like that, a little more, keep going.

I want demands and orders. Deeper, faster, slower, harder, rougher. Fuck me, eat me, hold me down, say my name, use your fingers, give me that cock, Malcolm.

I want gasping pleas. Don't stop don't you fucking stop, I'm so close, make me come.

Have you come? I think you have. What do you think about when you do? How do you touch yourself? Would you teach me every secret or just set me loose, make me learn to play you from scratch?

What do you want to hear from me?

I'm noisy in bed. I earn furtive shushings from shy lovers and angry thumps from neighbors who've shared walls with me.

You can have every whisper and mounting moan and grunt and panting breath, every curse, every uncensored thought, be it needy or bossy or pleading or plain old lust-drunk.

I'd tell you kiss me, stroke me, taste me, use me, ride me, suck me, spread your legs, make me come.

I'd be any man for you. Every man. Any man you've ever wanted, just tell me and I can be that. You can submit to me, exploit me, worship me, degrade me. I don't care as long as it leaves you trembling and weak.

Then I'll kiss your temple, taste the sweat gleaming on that skin. Kiss your lips, taste myself there.

Do you forgive me, stranger, for being so ungrateful, so foolish and naive to have almost tried to end all of this? Tell me how to make it up to you. Tell me who you want me to be, and I'll tell you exactly what that could look like.

4.44am

If you want to stop, stop.

Because I promise, it's only going to get worse from here.

This, right now, is me holding back. This is me deleting dirtier things, and putting sweeter things in their place. It's me censoring myself, in case it's too far or too much. Oh, I so don't want to be too much. But the problem is—I'm first seeing fresh water after a million miles of sea voyage.

I can't stop myself if we continue.

So please say now.

Don't tell me to make you my whore.

I will.

Don't ask me to degrade you.

It would be my pleasure.

I'm already worshipping your body in my head—each part of it a roulette that nightly lands on a different shape or size or softness. Sometimes you're hard all over, like a long-distance runner after a thousand-mile race. Sometimes you're as plump as a pillow and twice as juicy, or fine-boned like a bird or better than all of those things.

And I'm always glad to get any of them.

My teeth ache at the thought of biting.

My lips buzz with the idea of kissing.

I've come at least once every day since the first sensual word you said—about your hands, I think it was your hands, oh I think about your hands all the time—and I'll keep on doing it.

Unless you say: go back, let's be how we were, I'm weary in my bones and I need you to be more than this. Because I can be. I can forget we ever said a single sexual word and return to those conversations about songs and shows and food. You tell me about your day, and I'll tell you about mine.

But you have to make that decision.

I'm way too far gone to ever do it.

5.03am

Here's the deal, stranger. From 7am to 10pm, we talk about our days. TV, the weather, what we're eating. But between those stretches, anything goes.

Anything.

Don't hold back. I want to hear. I want to know everything you need from me so I can imagine being that man. I'm so fucking hard right now from reading your words. I ache all over at the thought of pleasing you.

Do you want to picture me better? If you'd prefer to keep me generic and changeable, skip my next text.

Let's see… I'm almost tall, not quite six feet. Brown eyes, dark brown hair. I wear reading glasses now and then. I'd like to think I'm fit. I can't jog anymore, but I do what I can. I've lost some weight since I moved here, and my skin's gone pale under all these clouds. I look tired, if I'm honest. At any given moment, I'm probably wearing jeans, and just now I've got a sweater on, dark greenish blue. A gray thermal beneath that. Boxer briefs, also gray, sometimes black. Bare feet. Some chest hair, not a ton.

I've got more I could tell you. Darker shadows to illuminate, but I'll let context lead us there in time.

So easily I could send you a picture. Of my face. Of my cock. A video. I could call you, hear your voice and let you hear mine.

But we're not going to do that, are we? We haven't yet, and we won't, I can feel it. I can tell from the way we text. How we take turns, and take our time with these pseudo letters.

Something about this is so exactly right as it is. Like we're two ghosts whispering in the darkness.

So tell me where I am. In your bed, on your floor? Kneeling before you, looming above, lounging across your covers or lashed to your bedposts? Still dressed or stripped bare? Don't leave anything out. Don't hold back. Tell me everything.

5.47am

That deal is okay with me.

As long as it's okay with you.

I don't want to hurt you. Make things worse for you. Pull apart your comfort zone when you need it most. These messages should be your comfort zone, and if they ever stray away from that I want you to tell me. Even now, after you've said that I should go ahead.

Though god, I want to go ahead. I was beside myself at you saying "so fucking hard", and then you went and described what you look like. All those words that I sort of didn't want to read, and yet somehow I started and couldn't stop. I devoured your dark brown hair and your reading glasses and your not a ton of chest hair.

Even the clothes made me push a hand between my legs.

And the don't hold back just sealed the deal.

Now I'm typing this with one thumb, body thrumming, fingers teasing in all the good good places as I think about where I would like you to be. Though most of the time, I find I can hardly decide. I think about you lounging on my bed, mostly bare, expression full of all the experiences I've never had, and my clit jumps against my fingers.

But there's something tempting about you dropping to your knees, too.

Burying your face between my legs, hungrily.

Hands spread over my ass.

Mouth already seeking me out.

Can you see yourself doing that, Malcolm?

If not, let me help you. Imagine finding me in the middle of my sparsely decorated living room, in nothing but an oversized jumper. It always slides off one shoulder, and grazes the tops of my knees. My legs are bare, soft, short, like the stalks of some succulent plant that's been starved of the sun. My thighs kiss in the middle.

I have no underwear on.

And when you press your face there, you'll find I have no hair between my legs, either. I keep myself smooth as silk there—made smoother by my own constant wetness. Because I am now, you know. Constantly wet, I mean. I wake up from sultry dreams filled with seething bodies, soaked all the way down to the tops of my thighs. When I walk around my apartment, I can feel it; when I slide a finger inside myself, it's easy.

Do you like the thought of it being easy?

Of putting your hand there and finding me slippery?

I like to think you would—that you would jolt all over and look up at me, shocked to discover that such an innocent little thing could be so aroused. But then I wonder if it would just spoil any illusions about me and the kind of person I am. Maybe you thought that closing myself off from everything meant that I had never fully learned how to crave.

And yet when I think of you looking at me like I should be ashamed…

Somehow that only makes me want to be worse. It sends a shudder through my body. Suddenly my cheeks are flushed to the point of unbearable. And most importantly: my finger is moving fast now on my clit. So fast, in fact, that I'm going to have to leave you there, to see to it.

I've only got enough good sense left to ask:

Which of those men would you be, Malcolm?

Forget what I want. Tell me who you are.

6.21am

You can't hurt me, stranger. There's ugliness in my everyday life and there's ugliness in sex, but one starves me while the other fills me up. So never fear. There's so much light in the dark places you want to go with me.

I don't even know where to start with the things you said. I want to do ten thousand things to you, but I have to pick, now don't I?

Fuck, you and your jumper. The fact that I had to Google "jumper British def" to even be sure what it meant. I thought it was a dress, but no.

I picture a man's sweater, overlong, falling off your shoulder like you said. I imagine it's mine. I imagine coming home and finding you in my living room. I don't know who you are, only that you're there in my apartment, dressed in my sweater with your bare, plump, porcelain legs, birdlike hands, wide eyes. They grow wider as I come near. Even I don't know what I'll do until I'm doing it.

I ask who you are. You don't answer, lips pursed tight. (What do those lips look like? Tell me. I'd give anything to know.)

My question becomes a demand, and you say you're nobody.

In truth, I don't care who you are. All I care about is that you're here, and you're mine to do with as I please.

I take a step closer. Too close. You take a step back. Step for step, until your calves hit the couch and you fall, land with a soft bounce on the center cushion.

I like the sight of you staring up at me with that mix of fear and anticipation in your stone-blue eyes.

A hundred ideas flash through my mind for what to do with you.

To you.

I want to undo my belt, open my pants. Take my cock out and make you watch as I stroke myself, get myself hard, until that pale flesh flushes dark. Until you can see the excitement beading, cresting, slipping from my crown, then gleaming along my shaft as that hand keeps on pumping.

I want to beckon you forward to the edge of your seat, guide my cock to your chin, watch it disappear between your lips. Watch your face as I feed you every inch, as you taste a man's desire for the first time.

I want to feel your inexperience in those awkward, eager, nervous seconds.

Your shy hands hide in your lap. I grasp your wrist, make you wrap your fingers around me and show you how tight I want it, show you how hard you make me. Show you how to stroke me so your rising fist meets your swallowing lips. Let you hear the way my breath sucks in with each pull. Make you feel the weight of my hand on your head and the soft tug of my fingers in your hair. I won't force you, just follow the bobbing of your head.

But that's only one idea, stranger, and not what really happens.

Not this night, anyway.

What really happens is that I take you by the hand. Coax you to stand with all the airs of a gentleman inviting you to waltz. As you rise, I turn you around, hold you by the waist, then draw you down onto my lap, your back meeting my chest.

You feel my mouth on your neck—the cool, smooth tip of my nose, the harsh rasp of my jaw. As I kiss your throat, my hands sweep over your body from your shoulders down over your breasts, your belly, your thighs.

You can feel that I'm hard, feel me pressing there against your ass, but there's no details to catch hold of, and you want the details so, so badly.

My fingers close around the hem of that stolen sweater and tug it up to your hips. Though I can't see what greets me, I feel it. I don't let you see the shock as my fingers traverse your skin—smooth, smooth, always smooth. Not what I expect from someone so sheltered. Maybe you hear the way my breath halts, or maybe your own gasp keeps my surprise a secret.

The edge of my finger meets your slick, soft folds. So wet I have to wonder what it is you thought about as you waited for a stranger to come home and find you here. Catch you.

I trace you with my knuckles, let you feel my rough skin against your soft lips. I stroke you like that for ages, waiting. Waiting for you to beg. To admit you want more.

Maybe you don't tell me in words. Maybe it's your panting breaths that tell me. Or the fingers that curl around my wrist to ride the motions, to feel the flex of my tendon and bone. Maybe it's the moan that finally escapes your throat. Whatever the case, I finally end your suffering.

I give you my fingers. Two of them, only deep enough to tease. You make it so easy, like you said. You make me feel needed like I haven't in years. Maybe not ever. You make me feel powerful, strong, big beyond reason. I want to give you my cock, so badly you can never, ever understand what torture that need is like to live with. I want to hold your hips and make you sink down on it, glacier-slow.

I don't, though. Not tonight.

Tonight you get those fingers. Three of them now, and deeper. Deeper and thicker, enough to help you imagine what you're missing. My other fingers frame your pussy, and my thumb sweeps low, steals some of that wetness, brings it to your clit.

Does it take an hour to make you come? Does it take a single breath?

Whatever it takes, I'll give you that. The raw drag of my kisses, the slick friction of my thumb and the steady fucking of my fingers until you come apart in my lap. Shaking, shuddering. Groaning. I keep going until the pleasure crests past relief and into pain and that hand on my wrist is tugging, pleading for me to stop.

And I do. I stop, and there's just us. Two strangers in my lonely living room, and the smell of you everywhere.

And here I'll leave you. The boy will be awake soon, though there's nothing I want more than to lie here and wait for the buzz of my phone in this dark room. But this is bordering on addiction now, so I'll power it off, like a drunk pouring the last of his gin down the sink.

But there's always the next night, stranger. There's always another bottle, another taste. Another temptation I'm too helpless to pass up. So go on, then. Intoxicate me.

7.12am

I think I held my breath through your entire reply. Mostly because it was so hot my skin is now on fire, but also because I never thought I'd ever have anyone say things like that to me. Things that make me wild for them. Things that make me moan.

Things that fill me with joy.

Oh so much joy, just to see the way I seem through your eyes. You've never even looked at me, never heard anything but my own nervous descriptions, and yet you take them and turn them into something amazing. I sound so different, coming from you.

Like someone capable of being sexy.

Now the saggy jumper is yours, worn so I could smell you throughout the day. My little legs are porcelain; my eyes are wide. I get to be smooth beneath your fingers, and something like torture to you. Is it all right if I enjoyed being a sort of torture? Because I did, I have, I do. I read that one word and said your name, breathless and desperate.

And I only got more lascivious from there.

I made myself come twice—first from the thought of you showing me how you like it, how much you'd want me to suck you, how good you could make it for me with just your fingers, and then from the idea of what I'd do in return.

You have to know that I would do something in return.

That I could never leave you like that, with your cock all hard against my ass and my wetness still on your fingers. The need to make you feel as good would be too great; it was too great after reading, when I stroked myself to my second orgasm. It filled my head with all kinds of imaginings: like sliding down off your lap and onto my knees.

Lips swollen from that long, slow suck of your cock.

Tongue greedy to taste you.

Already begging for you to show me how you like it again, just so I can feel your fingers wrapped around mine as I work you.

So I get a hand on my head, urging me to go faster or slower or ohhhh god I want to come again just thinking about it.

Just thinking about you letting me know exactly what you need.

Tell me exactly what you need, Malcolm. Don't hold back. Fill in all the blanks in my inexperienced imagination.

9.31am

Oh, stranger. The things I want to say to you.

But you see there are rules now, and as it's between the hours of 7am and 10pm, I will keep it clean. I will tell you about my plans for the day and act as though your texts didn't pitch me into a fever dream.

After ten, I will tell exactly what I thought of them, and some ideas of my own. But not a minute before then.

Tell me about your day. Your plans. What will you read and watch and eat?

Me, I have set myself a mission. I was scrolling back through our texts and noticed I'd complained that I can't go running anymore. Toddlers aren't famous for their pace-setting or endurance, you see.

But I was wrong, I realized. People run all the time with kids. I just need a jogging stroller.

So that's what I'm doing with my day. I'll be bundling the boy up and driving us to Birmingham, where the internet has it on good authority that I might find a sporting goods store.

I'm a little nervous. For starters, I've only driven here maybe five times, never frequently enough to get used to the left-hand thing. The boy's made a quasi-hermit of me.

More to the point, I feel awkward out in public with him. The way he is... I always worry some well-meaning old woman will ask if he's okay, and I'll have no idea what to say, since he's not. I'd probably mumble something about him needing a nap, then get very interested in the check-out aisle magazines. I worry he looks so glazed that someone will assume I've drugged and abducted him.

But those fears won't deter me. We will find our stroller and a new pair of running shoes for me and afterward stop for ice cream, if I can find a place.

I wish I could buy us a Frisbee or a ball to toss around, but I tried the whole catch thing once, and I still cringe whenever I think of it.

I found a cricket ball when we were at the park and threw it to the boy. Not hard at all, just underhand, from a few feet away. I tossed it toward his chest, and instead of trying to catch it he turned away—swiveled from the knees and let it bounce off his arm—then just stood there frozen, face screwed up tight like a fist. Like he'd been hit by something before and was waiting for the next one.

I think it's for the best that I don't know exactly what he went through before I got here. That ignorance spares me knowing who I might need to track down and kick the living shit out of, and that's probably good. My energies are needed elsewhere.

Anyhow, that's my day. It sounds quite wholesome, don't you think?

Maybe later I'll tell you if we're successful.

And maybe later, sometime after 10pm, I'll tell you a few other things.

9.55am

I drifted off while waiting for your next message, thinking I was bound to wake up to something amazing. That it would make my impatience easier to bear.

Damn you, damn you, damn you.

Not a day in, and I already want to toss the rules to the wind.

But I won't, I promise I won't. Mostly because I respect your boundaries, and partly because I love to hear you talk about your day almost as much as whatever seediness we've descended into. Just knowing that you're choosing these things, wanting these things, beginning fresh with so many lovely activities…

It fills me with warmth. It makes me want to be brave too.

Because those things are brave, in my opinion. Every step you take with him must seem like a leap in the dark, and yet you're trying all the same. And though it might seem like your efforts are in vain, I know he hears you. I know he will feel the care you're taking.

It just takes time to show someone that there is more to life than whatever pain and misery they've suffered. To shift that paradigm inside them and undo all the terrible patterns that have been sewn through their soul.

But I have faith you'll get there.

You get me there.

Today, I stood out on my balcony. Just for a minute, but a minute is forever for me. By the time I crawled back inside, I was a wet rag, and not just from the thought of someone seeing me. It was the noise that really struck me, the incredible and all-consuming noise—even though I'm twenty floors up and only dared to do it at seven in the morning.

There were hardly any cars and no people walking past, and yet it felt like the world was roaring at me.

But you want to know the strangest part?

I liked that it did.

2.12pm

Your texts came through as I was getting the boy ready for our mission.

My phone was in my back pocket, and I felt every one of them, counted them. Thirteen. Like the chiming of the clock, buzz buzz buzz as I got him into a jacket, down the stairs, out to the car and into the Houdini-proof puzzle known as a car seat, then buzz buzz buzz from the cup holder as I drove us through the village toward the highway.

Sorry, motorway.

I wanted to check my phone. So, so badly. It must be how teenagers feel, this compulsion to snatch up a device and stare at a screen. Or how some of my friends back home could be. I was never like that. I always thought I was too cool for all that mindless scrolling, for obsessive app-checking.

Now, though. I bet I would have sneaked a peek while I was driving if not for the boy. And if not for how hard I have to concentrate, what with the alien signage and clockwise roundabouts.

But I was strong. I didn't check when I parked. I didn't check as we waited in line at the store with our prize. (You'll never guess how expensive jogging strollers are.) I didn't check as I sat across from the boy while he stared at his ice cream melting in its plastic bowl.

I didn't check until just now, with him down for a nap and the dishes washed and the stroller manual read. I'm quite impressed with myself.

Though that doesn't change the fact that you're clearly my Candy Crush or whatever digital crack people are forsaking their loved ones and livelihoods over these days.

I read your texts, and I won't lie—I cried.

Only a little, but yeah, I cried like a little bitch. Over the words I'd asked you before not to say to me, about hanging in there and how I'm doing the right thing or whatever.

About him hearing me, because I really, really hope he does.

Before, I couldn't have heard those encouraging words. Not without dismissing them, thinking them as sweet and empty as aspartame. We really were strangers then, stranger. But coming from you now, they mean a lot.

And the part where you told me what you did, about going out on your balcony...

Oh, Christ, that was the end of me. The most pathetic and homely sound fell out of my mouth, like an ehhgghn from the top of my throat, and I cried way more. It was so sudden and so alarming, and I tried to rub the tears away like they were wasps. I don't know who I was afraid would see.

Why cry at all, though? Why not jump up and pump a fist toward the ceiling in triumph, because HOLY SHIT THAT IS A BIG FUCKING DEAL YOU'RE AMAZING.

Don't get me wrong, I was seriously proud of you. But I think it was humility I was feeling, or some kind of personal pride that made me cry. Because I think you're saying that I had something to do with you deciding to do that, to step out on that balcony and let the world roar its silence at you, and I'm not sure I've ever been that for someone. Whatever the word is.

"Inspiring" sounds so fucking narcissistic.

"Motivating" is just douchey.

But whatever it is, it made me cry to think I could be that for somebody. I don't know if I was crying because that felt so good, to be that for you, or because I was ashamed to have never been that for anyone before now.

Anyhow, there's my dark and tortured masculine mystique shot to shit. Never fear, I'll get it together by the time 10pm rolls around.

Right. Two bites of ice cream does not a well-balanced lunch make, so I better figure something out before the boy wakes up.

Later, I'll be rereading your texts from early this morning.

And figuring out precisely what it is I want to do with you next.

In the meantime, tell me about your childhood.

I'm not asking for a banquet here, just a few forkfuls. What was your first pet, or what was the view out of your bedroom window? Did you like to jump in puddles, and if so, what color were your boots?

Anything. Anything at all.

3.33pm

Now I don't know whether to be happy or annoyed at myself. I forgot that you had asked me not to give you any hang-in-theres. The urge to tell you how amazing I think you're doing just took over my fingers, and I couldn't seem to do anything about it.

Call it excitement over the balcony.

Adrenaline or something.

Though I'd be a liar if I said I didn't love knowing that it was encouraging in some way. That they made you feel so much, and part of the feeling was pride. Because you should be proud.

Of what you're doing for him. Of what you're doing for me.

You are doing something for me, Malcolm. I don't know what it is either, but I can tell it's there. I wake up more hopeful about what the day might bring. More excited about my life, because now I know my life can have something in it. I can talk to someone without smashing to pieces and feel pleasure without following it up with guilt or shame.

Even the thought of you going away doesn't terrify me like I thought it would.

Though I hope you take that the right way.

I don't ever want you to feel like I couldn't be without you.

But oh, I would love you to stay.

3.44pm

Damn, I keep skipping your questions. I got as far as thirty seconds into MasterChef before I realised. But in my defense, there always seems to be so much to say. It's easy to miss things out, even if I don't mean to.

Or maybe I mean to a little, when it comes to childhood.

Even though your questions brought up so many sweet memories. I had red wellingtons, as bright and glossy as glace cherries. And I loved them so much that I actually hated puddles. I avoided them so my lovely boots could stay looking so pretty. No marks on them, no streaks of mud. Just two perfect little jewels, always waiting for me by the front door.

Instead of the usual series of hand-me-downs and things worn to a thread.

And I never had a pet.

Pretty glad about that now.

What about you? Tell me your favourite thing from childhood.

6.22pm

I should have known better than to ask.

With every question, I keep expecting to learn something about you, to get a solid, tangible answer I can hold in my hands, a new shard of a vessel I'm trying to piece together to contain you.

But every answer only hatches a hundred more questions and leaves you somehow more nebulous than ever. Like maybe this pot is as big as a pyramid, and even a bathtub full of shards can't help me.

That's not a criticism, though. I'm not annoyed, and I'm not going to pry. Not just yet. For now, I'll take what I can get and turn your eerie, beautiful, melancholy little details this way and that in the light, and enjoy them for the puzzle pieces they are.

As for me, my favorite thing from childhood...

I have a lot. I have tons.

I could say my grandma's pool.

I could say Super Mario Kart.

I could say driving out near Sandia in the middle of the night to watch meteor showers.

I could say a hundred things, but looking back it's hard not to say my mom. Maybe that's because I lost her a couple years ago, or maybe it's simply because she's there, in just about every good memory I have. Even Mario Kart. (She was always Donkey Kong, which I thought was pretty badass for a girl.)

I had a happy enough childhood. My parents were married, and they did a decent job. It was just me, no siblings, but they didn't spoil me.

My dad and I were never super close. He's not a bad guy, just one of those men who struggle to relate to kids. Even his own. He's...odd. Even as a child I knew it. I worried when I was younger that I might be weird like him, like I could inherit it the way I had his eyes. Probably has everything to do with my old need to pass for cool.

But we did have good times. He's an astronomy nerd, so he's the one who wanted to drive out to the mountains at one in the morning on a school night to see the meteors or a lunar eclipse or whatever planet was orbiting extra close to the Earth. I was mostly in it for the hot chocolate and some bank shot facsimile of his attention, but I liked it okay, too.

It always felt like his telescopes were way more interesting to him than me, but he didn't land me in therapy or anything. And I can still identify a fuckload of constellations, which has got to be a dying art.

Since my mom died, he and I almost never talk, if only because we got lazy, relying on her to pass the phone and spur our few yearly conversations. I call on his birthday and Father's Day, but to be honest, I'm always a little relieved if it goes to voicemail and I can just leave a message.

It's embarrassing how little we have to say to each other. Sometimes I wonder if he maybe has Asperger's. It would make me feel better to find out he's awkward with me because of that and not because there's something inherently broken about us as a unit.

But my mom was amazing. I'd say my best childhood memory was the day I woke up and she told me I was sick.

She just announced I was "sick" and that I didn't have to go to school, and that we could do anything I wanted for the entire day.

I was really young, so it probably bleeds over into other memories, but I know for sure I asked for water balloons. There's nothing as good as pelting your mom with a water balloon. And I know we went to McDonald's and she let me order off the grown-up menu, and I got the meal with two cheeseburgers.

That was the day I saw Indiana Jones and the Last Crusade in the theater, even though she had to know it was way too scary for a seven-year-old. My friends were all so jealous. It was righteous, as we said in those days.

Looking back, I wonder if that happened just after she got sick for the first time. It would have been the same year, I think. She always got a little impulsive and sort of... aggressively fun when there was a recurrence. Maybe my sick day was actually her sick day.

I wish she was here, so so badly. Alive, of course, but also here, with me. I wish the boy could meet her. I wish she'd be here five years from now, when he's seven, to inform him he's sick and take him out to some righteously age-inappropriate matinee in the middle of a school day.

That's probably my biggest wish. What's yours, stranger?

Talk again once the boy's asleep. I've got a penne bake to assemble and a toddler to bathe and bedtime songs to sing to the world's least enthusiastic audience.

6.55pm

I feel terrible for not wanting to talk about it a lot—of not knowing how to talk about myself a lot—because I love hearing your details so much. I just want to go over all of them and ask you what this one felt like and what happened after that. But it doesn't seem fair when I only offer shards in return.

So I'm going to try. Maybe start with Mario Kart.

Because oh I love love loved it too. I was only friends with a girl in my year so I could play it. And I was good at it. I could nail anyone with a green shell or a banana—and I was never ever sorry. In fact, it was the one thing that I didn't care about hurting feelings over.

Feel my blue shell of death you turd licker was a common refrain of mine, for those afternoons at Lindy Potter's house.

Man, I lived for those afternoons.

I would have probably lived for afternoons at your house, too. Playing games and eating burgers and water balloon fights. Even the stargazing sounds amazing—all of it like all of my daydreaming about being a kid in some warm American suburb. Back then I devoured films and books about ballparks and bubblegum and picket fences. I was Ramona Quimby and Stacey from the Baby-Sitters Club.

Hell, I was the murdered girl in a Point Horror novel over being myself. Being dead there seemed infinitely better than being alive where I ended up.

Though of course I know none of that's really true. I totally get that it was just a fantasy, and the reality isn't any different. Or at least the pain isn't any different when something terrible happens. I can't imagine what it must be like to have had those things with your Mom and then lose her. Or to be so close to something like a great relationship with your Dad, and then so far.

I don't know if I would want it, knowing that it could be so easily taken away.

I'm so sorry you had to go through it.

Can that be my wish, to wish you hadn't?

9.54pm

That's just how it is, I guess. Good things come, and eventually they leave us. Or sometimes we leave them first. Sometimes we even get a chance to say goodbye.

A part of me wants to promise you that I'll never leave, that I'll always pick up this phone, but only a liar can make that promise. I could be hit by a bus tomorrow. I could waste away from cancer when I'm sixty-two. I can only be here now.

That's something I have to say to myself a lot these days— that I'm here now.

I lug a lot of shame around, knowing I didn't come over the second I found out I had a son. I knew about him for seven months before I came. Knowing what I do now, it's like a knife between my ribs.

If I'd come, and if I'd seen what state he's in. I could have spared him seven months of only god knows what. Seven months it might take him seven extra years of therapy to get over, for all anyone knows.

But there's no such thing as time machines, and, in the end, no such thing as wishes, so all I've got is that mantra. I'm here now.

I do have my dad to credit for one thing—he's making me a better father, myself. If only because I'm determined to give the boy what my dad couldn't seem to give me. I'm always on the floor, on the grass. Always itchy to show him I'm here, let's play. Let's do kid stuff. Let's do you stuff. Whatever that might be.

I'm living for the day he comes over while I'm messing with his blocks or his toy bulldozer and finally decides to join in. I have to believe it'll happen. If I didn't, I don't think I could get out of bed.

Okay, stranger, this is heavy shit. But you know what? It's after ten. I'm going to leave you momentarily to pour myself a drink and reread your message from earlier, reset my head. And after that, I promise I'll make it worth the wait.

10.15pm

You said it thrilled you, the idea of torturing me. Can I confess something, stranger?

You already are.

I'm suffering. I haven't come since before we first discovered each other. Not even with your fantasies setting me on fire, getting me hotter than anything I've ever read or seen or heard or felt before.

I couldn't.

I nearly did any number of times, but then…

I didn't want to come, then find your words still glowing on my screen in the aftermath, seeming utilitarian as porn. I couldn't bear to cheapen them like that. They mean too much.

And perhaps even more than that, I haven't wanted the ache to end.

How does that make you feel, to know I'm so hard and so frustrated it physically hurts? That you've done that to me. That you're the only one who can fix it.

I know how it makes me feel. Helpless. Alive. Desperate. Electric.

All thanks to you.

So what I want is this—come back to the fantasy with me. Where we left off, after I made you come.

I want you on my lap, eager and frantic, only face to face this time. I want to feel you claim me, easing down slowly, savoring. Discovering what it feels like, taking a man inside you.

I want to think you're about to end my torment, to feel the slick, flushed heat of you working me, to revel in the fact that I made you this lush and tight, and now I'm about to claim my reward.

I assume it's my turn. That it's only a matter of time. That you're an angel, sent to save me from this hurt.

Then you put your lips to my ear, and you say, "You don't come until I tell you to."

Something moves through me at those words, a shiver made of fire. A fever as cold as ice. I don't understand. You're riding me hard, and I'm so close. It's been days and days and days and I'm so. Fucking. Close. I say, "What?"

"Don't you dare come until I say you can."

I always knew we were playing a game, stranger, but the rules have changed. You've changed. There's mischief and cruelty in your voice, and it has me as hot as the waiting or the strokes of your pussy or the smell of your own satisfaction in this room.

I want nothing more than to lose control, end this maddening ache. Grab your hips and force the motions, quench my cock and shoot you full of me, make a mess of the both of us.

But even more than that…I want to be obedient.

I know you've got more in store for me. Your hands or your mouth, your words and your plans for my suffering.

You're going to test me, and I can't guess what the punishment could be for disappointing you.

I nearly want to find out.

But not as much as I want to please and abide by you.

I don't know, I don't know. My mind is on fire, and all I know for sure is how badly this hurts.

So now you go next.

Tell me how you'd test me.

10.48pm

You asked me who the fuck I am. The truth is—I don't know when you start talking about all this sex stuff. It's like a switch flicks inside me, and suddenly I'm filthier than I ever thought I could be. It's like my arousal has been walled up, and now you're poking holes in it. Cracks are starting to appear. Things are pouring through.

Like how much I want to do what you just told me to.

How did you know that I would want to do what you just told me to?

I read the words couldn't and hurt and don't you dare and test, and my body went wild. I had to stop before I returned your text, just so I could properly control the things I said.

But I can feel them spilling out anyway. I want to make fists in your hair—hold you there while I take what I need. Then just as you get desperate, just as you're ready to beg, I would stop. Maybe pull those handfuls until you're not sure if it hurts or thrills you.

I think it would thrill you.

Tell me that it would thrill you.

Tell me that you would beg me to continue, and when I did that you would just want me to stop. I can almost hear the words it's way too much, hissed between your gritted teeth. See you panting and shivering with long held back pleasure. Hear you gasping as you fight for some control.

But I don't want you to control yourself, my Malcolm.

I want you to break down. Be a mess for me.

Is it wrong to want you to be a mess for me?

I don't know. I don't know. I think it's better if I don't say.

You say now, instead.

10.57pm

Yes, it thrills me. All of it. Every last word. Every single fucking goddamn pixel.

It thrills me to know I have that power to tear holes in your armor. Thrills me to surrender that power in the same breath and kneel cowering before you, happy to beg.

Thrills me to think about those fists in my hair. To think of you using my body.

Thrills me beyond reason to see you call me yours. Your Malcolm.

Thrills me to imagine being the mess you so want to see, the one you must ache to reduce me to as badly as I ache for the relief. Handy how those two desires dovetail, don't you think?

But before I tell you exactly how it is you break me down and rip me apart, finally end all of this torture, I have one final question for you.

You have to answer it.

You can lie, but you have to answer.

The thing is,

I'm hurting.

I'm desperate.

I'm begging.

Yet I don't even know whose feet I'm cowering at.

And so my question is,

what's your name?

11.18pm

Is that the price I have to pay before you tell me? The toll before I get to go down that road of ripping and tearing and whatever else you want me to do? I'd say that seems unfair, but I know it isn't. I don't even know why I haven't told you. What makes me hold back things.

Tell me your name.

Oh god. I don't think I can talk to you like this. I don't think I can do this.

Yes, you can. Tell me your name.

Things were so good as they were!

And they can be good like this, too. Tell me your name.

I want to. I feel like maybe this is what I need, this fast. No time to think. No time to lie.

So tell me your name, and we can start.

Maya. It's Maya.

Maya. Maya. I'm saying it aloud. Hearing it in this still room. Feeling it on my tongue.

How does it taste, then?

Like the rain. Is it raining there, like it is here?

Yes. Pouring it down. When I press my cheek against the glass, it's practically vibrating.

Where is this window? Above your couch? Your bed?

Above my couch. But I had the urge to lie then and say bed.

I think you know what I'm going to ask of you next.

I do, but I need to see you say it.

I won't ask yet. First, I'll tell you I'm in my chair. The one I dragged over to sit before the radiator. I'm there, with my bare feet and my clinking glass, and the cool breeze coming in, and the sound of the rain. Sounds just like your name.

I can see it. Do you want to see me, too?

Always.

I'm sprawled on my couch. I have to sprawl; I can't sit up. I've gone weak all over just because we're talking like this. Just because I picture you so clearly. And I want you to picture me clearly, in return. I'm only wearing a T-shirt, and knickers.

That made me smile. Knickers. That makes me sound about eight instead of thirty-four, but there you go.

This is strange, isn't it? Or rather, talking like this isn't strange at all. What's strange is how it's taken us so long to get here. To text like normal people.

I almost said panties. But that wouldn't be me. And yes, it is strange. Strange that I don't feel as scared as I thought I would, talking to you so directly. It's easier than it should be.

I wonder what it says about us that we took a medium designed for haste and abbreviation and smiley faces and back-and-forth-and-back-and-forth and used it the same way we might carrier pigeons or letters sealed with wax. That we're scared? Or perhaps that there's some pleasure to be found in the composing? The crafting and curating of thoughts until they're just so, worthy of offering?

Or perhaps it's the waiting. Anticipating.

I thought it was fear. But now I don't know. The need for editing seems so silly in light of how easy this is. It makes me wonder more about that one sweet word: anticipation. I can't deny that I've gone to sleep full of excitement at the thought of what might be waiting for me when I wake.

Now I feel like Santa.

The world's grown very instantaneous, hasn't it? We want everything now, right now.

Maybe we were meant for a different era. Parchment and quills and seven oceans standing between us. Carriages caught in the rain and boiling-over words said too soon for fear that they will be the last ones. Like Beethoven: my thoughts turn to you, my immortal beloved.

Very romantic, stranger. Very poetic. Very you. Makes me wish my fingers were stained with ink.

I wish for other things, too. Now that we're not editing… If you were here, I wouldn't want to feel you, edited. No going back, exing out a fumbling touch or a messy first meeting of our mouths.

You wouldn't. I don't think I could edit myself if I were there or you were here. The second you said fingers stained with ink I thought about them on me, making patterns over my skin.

My brain wants to come up with some clever, poetic simile involving Rorschach tests, but my body's too overheated and impatient to give many shits about cleverness.

I wasn't lying when I said I've waited. That it's been days. Over a week.

It's been since before we first met.

Then be impatient with me. Show me what a week of torture has done.

I'm bringing you into my room. Hang on.

Shall I tell you about it? My room?

You can, but if I were there I wouldn't pay any attention. Every inch of my focus would be on you.

Then I'll give you just one detail: the window's open. Just above the head of my bed. If you want to feel that, you know what to do.

I was already laid beneath it before you said a word. I can practically feel the rain on my bare skin as I lie there waiting for you.

Good. I'm on my bed now. I'm going to undo my belt. I think you'd like to know about it, my belt. That's a detail you'd want, like how you might want to know what the wrapper of a candy looks like before you open it, what color, and is it metallic or striped, does it crinkle? So I'll tell you. It's just old, worn, dark brown leather. Thick and cracked. Silver buckle. Nothing fancy.

Nothing fancy just made me flush hot all over. I can see you with that buckle in your hands. Hear it clink. Hear the slow slide of leather.

You're exactly right. Such a small sound, the rain just about swallows it, but you wouldn't miss it, would you? You drink up that tiny nothing-sound, leather sighing through metal.

I'd tell you about my jeans, next. How I'd undo the button, and about another tiny sound, the one the zipper would make. But if you were here, I have to imagine it'd be your fingers there. Fumbling and eager.

I'm so primed, I think I can hear your heart beating from here. I doubt there's any sound that could escape me, but that zipper...

oh if I heard that zipper. I don't think I could stop myself from pushing your hands away. From finishing it off myself.

Jesus, you're sexy.

You've never touched a man before, have you? Not in any way?

Is the sexy part that I haven't, or that I'm so greedy anyway?

Both. Neither. It's just you. How you are. You're ten thousand things, and I can't predict a one of them.

Part of me thinks I should pretend I'm demure. But I'm doing my best to give you the truth. To tell you that I wouldn't stop with the zipper—in my head I've already divested you of most of your clothes.

Pity for you, here in reality we're still poised to deal with the zipper. Let me tell you a couple of things.

I'm hard. It's dim in this room, there's just the streetlight slipping through the window, but you might be able to tell. Or see enough to think you can tell, but you're not sure. Not until your fingers are on that zipper, sliding it down slow. Then there'd be no mistaking it.

Your knuckles would brush me, and the whole of my body would twitch and buck, and my breath would come up short. Would yours do the same?

So you want to torture me in return? Good. Good. Yes, my breath would come up short. If I felt you and knew that you were in that state, if I brushed you and you bucked into my eager hands…I don't think I would breathe for a week. I'm not breathing now.

What's anticipation if not torture with a prize at the end?

Talking with you like this is making me notice a thousand things I otherwise wouldn't. Like the way it feels, laying my palm over myself there. My open fly is soft—these jeans are ancient. There's the raspy edge of the zipper, the cool metal of the button quickly going warm from my hand. More softness, the cotton of my shorts. So much softness, but you know there's more. Heat and hardness. You can feel my pulse there, ticking in time with those heartbeats you were listening to.

If I took your hand and put it on me, what would I feel? Soft skin, I know that much. Any rings? Short nails, long ones? Tell me.

I wish they were long. I wish they were so you could feel a hint of them as I explore. But I want the reality of this, too, so I'll tell you. My hands are bare of rings; my nails are bitten down to nothing. My fingers are feverish on you, though. Quick and feverish, mapping out everything you've just exposed.

I don't wish for anything other than your hands, exactly as they are. You must feel so much in the tips. No nails there, protecting them like tiny umbrellas. No calluses like the ones that've stripped my fingertips of all sensation. If I ever caught myself wishing for your nails, to feel them raking my skin, I'll ask for your teeth instead. On my neck, my ear. Dragging down the length of my thumb.

Do you really think your thumb is where I want my mouth to be?

Now you'll have to picture me smiling, here in this dark room.

Very well, I can sense you're impatient. I'm tempted to tell you you have no idea what impatience feels like, but if I did it'd only be to make you wait a few seconds longer.

And wouldn't that just be so cruel?

Enough teasing, though. Your hand is on me. Your soft hand on my hard cock. I'd hold it there until neither was cooler or warmer than the other, just until it began to blur, the edge where one ends and the other starts. Then I'd guide you by the wrist, ease your palm low, then back up. Slow. Not light, but not rough either. Not yet. I'd make you take the measure of me, with that maddening sliver of my shorts still keeping me half-secret.

Would you try to rush? Try to slip your thumb beneath my fly, wrap those fingers around me? Or would you go still and curious and obedient and take only what I offered, nothing more?

I think you know the answer, but I'll tell you anyway. I'll tell you that I'd be breathless, flushed, desperate. That those things would make me try to push past the tiny little steps you want us to take.

But then, oh then I'd revel in you stopping me. Hold me back. Tell me I'm wicked for wanting to map out every inch of your cock with my hands and lips and tongue.

Because that's what I'd do, Malcolm. I'd want to taste you now. My hot breath would ghost over the soft material between you and me before you could stop me.

Oh, now that'll never do.

How can we both have come this far after all this time, only to rush? You, you've never done these things. Me, I feel as though I haven't, the way we talk about them. I've begun to doubt I've ever kissed a woman, or felt her hands, or tasted her skin. How can I have, when the things you say fade all my memories to nothing more than ashes?

Okay, enough poetry. Here's what happens, Maya.

I don't tell you you're wicked. I don't tell you a thing, in fact. I turn you onto your back, brace my body above yours, pin your hands to the bed above your head. Get one knee between yours, then the other. Edge them wider, driving your legs open. Then I lower down, center my cock there against you, with the tangle of my belt and my jeans, the hem of your overlong shirt, all of that maddening mess there between us, reducing me to one word. Hard.

No other details. You tried to rush, so you don't get those details yet. All you get for now is my weight and the feel of my excitement, muffled and dulled. The shackles of my hands. And my face above yours, smiling. Smiling to hide the fact that I'm aching so badly I could scream.

Do you want me to move now? Against you? Tell me, and I will.

Do you think muffled and dulled is a punishment? That the shackles of your hands make me sorry? They don't. My legs spread automatically the moment you said you were between them. I can practically feel you there, pressed hard against the swell of my sex. Every time I imagine you moving against me, I shiver. I rock, as if you're really here.

So yes. Yes. Please, yes.

Fuck. Fuck these pants.

Okay, picture them gone. Picture me kicking them away in a fit of annoyance, the whole effort a clumsy, frantic affair, then hear the clatter of the buckle hitting the floor. Because that's exactly what just happened, here in reality.

Better. Slightly better.

I'm back on top of you now. We can feel so much more. Just two flimsy layers between us. I press the length of my cock along your folds, tight, moving just enough. Enough to tease. Enough for you to feel every inch of me. Just that, only that, until something changes. Until the smooth hush of cotton on cotton changes, beginning to drag and pull. Because I want you wet. I want your clit as stiff as my cock, want you throbbing, just as I am. When we get you there, then we'll find out what comes next. But not a second before.

You don't have to want. I am wet. I was wet the moment you said you were between my legs, and I'm wetter still just hearing you talk about my clit and how stiff you'd like it to be.

It is, you know. I can almost feel my pulse beating there, and every time you give me one more tiny thing, one more delicious detail, it swells. I get a little slicker. The urge to touch myself gets a little harder to resist—but I will. My hands are still above my head, held there by you. My body is still spread out beneath yours, only touched by whatever you allow.

Waiting, waiting for whatever you want to come next.

What I want is you on your back. Is there a pillow? I want the edge of it between your legs. Or a blanket, twisted into a rope. I want to know there's some blunt facsimile of me there against your pussy, growing wet as your hips start to move, seeking the friction. Seeking me. Do that, and I'll give you more. Promise.

There's no need to promise. I was scrabbling for the nearest thick, firm thing before I finished reading your words. It's there now between my legs, solid enough that I can feel it without moving a muscle but oh god when I do…

I've made a mess of it already.

Christ, I swear I can smell you here. It must be seven hundred degrees in this clammy, drafty old room. I'm stripping my sweater and shirt away. That only leaves my underwear.

It'd be wrong to just shed those as well, though. So I bid you to get up. To leave the bed, kneel on the floor beside the heap of my abandoned clothes.

I join you on those cold floorboards, standing. Invite you to be free of the last stitch that stands between you and this thing you've been theorizing and fantasizing about for unnumbered years. Peel them down slowly or tear them to tatters, I don't care. Do it in a rush or touch me first—trace the length of me through that soft cotton. Whatever you want. Whatever you've been waiting for.

My hands would be on you quickly, pulling and tugging until you were bare. But once I was there, I'm not sure how I would be. Hesitant, breath catching, unsure if whatever I was doing is right? Or too aroused to hold back, mouth already following my hands, kissing whatever I revealed? I think it would be the latter. I think I'd damn the consequences, brave your laughter over any possible blunders. Let you feel how sloppy my eagerness makes me as I lick over the length of your cock. As I take you in my mouth before I'm ready, forgetting to breathe, almost choking, hands all over you all at once.

Fuck, Maya.

You make me feel so fucking…everything. Big. Hard. Desired, most of all. Alive and dirty and helpless and huge.

Forgive me, but fuck the fantasy. There's nothing left in my head but steam and colors. All I can give you is exactly what's happening. Tell you I'm naked, on my back on these rumpled covers, burning up in this cold, dark room. Tell you I've fisted myself, that I'm stroking myself, if barely. Just barely. I need this so badly. Just tell me how. Help me end this. Tell me to go fast, slow, tight, rough, light. Whatever you'd want to see. Tell me so I can get there. So you can get me there. Because I'm not going to last another minute.

Go fast. Go hard. Go like you can't stand it any longer.

Because I can't. I'm rutting against this pillow between my legs now, barely able to type. My whole body is shuddering, sweating, as flushed as I've ever been in my life. The ache between my legs is so strong I can hardly stand it. My teeth are gritted against it. I've never been able to come with so little direct contact, but I think it's going to happen now.

So make it happen for you, too. Make a fist so tight around your cock I could see the white of your knuckles if I was there. Stroke yourself quickly, like you need to come too bad to stop.

SUNDAY

1.03am

Are you there, stranger?

I'm here. Just. Maybe. God.

The rain's stopped. Nearly. I don't know when. I'm just growing cold atop the covers. The breeze is almost too much, or not nearly enough. I don't know.

I feel so much, and yet almost nothing at all. My body's not gone this quiet in months. Like I can hear every sound. The grass outside, dripping. The blood slowly creeping back through my veins. You, breathing who knows how many miles away.

Strange, because I've never felt so loud. It's like my insides are rushing to fill all the empty spaces up. I'm not surprised you can hear me—my heart is shouting in my chest.

Thank you. Thank you.

I don't know what to say aside from you're welcome. I don't even know what you're thanking me for… An orgasm? I don't think it's that. Maybe something too big to explain. That's how it feels to me, anyway. Though bear in mind, I just came so hard I very nearly died, so there's a lot of delirium at work.

But thank you, too.

Yes. Too big to explain. Too complicated to process.

Too much for me to talk about. If I do, I might say something ridiculous.

Your ridiculous, lust-addled thoughts are all the poetry I'll ever want for the rest of my life.

But it's late, stranger. And my body was so starved for that, it feels as though I'm wandering out into the larger world after years trapped in a cave. Like this screen's burning my eyes.

But more importantly, I know if I sleep now, I'll dream about you. If I dream. I hope I do, if you'll be there. So perhaps it's time to say goodnight, stranger.

Or rather, goodnight, Maya.

I'll see you in the morning.

Goodnight, my Malcolm. Don't worry about whether you'll dream of me.

I'm already there, with you.

5.19am

Are you there, stranger?

I hope not. I hope you're sound asleep, dreaming of me or of us, or perhaps not dreaming at all. Maybe just blessed blankness, like a starless night spread out beneath a new moon.

I should be dreaming, too, but I just had to write.

Something amazing's happened. Something so tiny but so amazing. It'll probably sound silly to even bother to say… Only no, not to you. You won't think it's silly at all.

I did dream of you, by the way. Not the sort of waking fever dreams I'd entertained earlier, not like that.

An odd and innocent dream, about getting up in the morning and finding you in my kitchen. In your shirt, or maybe it was the sweater. It was gray, and it fell to the tops of your thighs. You were at the sink, washing a mug. My mug, the one I always drink from, with its illustration of calla lilies, so faded only the blues are left, and there's a chip right where your lips want to be. My mom's old mug.

You were waiting for the kettle to boil. Your hair was down. It was long, darkish brown, wavy. Messy, like you'd just woken up. I think you had bangs. I don't know what we spoke of, if we did, or even what you looked like aside from your hair and that you smiled, and when you did it made your cheeks so round.

But then the boy woke me with his moans. I think it must have been just after three. I'd have guessed that would've been the worst, to be woken from such a pleasant and charming mystery by that call to duty, but you know what? It was fine.

For the first time ever, I felt prepared. I felt rested, bizarrely. Or my body felt at peace, some sweet strain of resignation. Is that the definition of surrender, I wonder?

I went to him as I always do. I propped him up on his bed, pulled him onto my crossed legs, and hugged him tight around the middle. Rocked him and told him it's okay. It's only a dream. I'm here. I sang to him. He went still a little quicker than usual, I think, after five songs. Half an album—halfway through Harvest, to be precise.

When he fell slack, I eased him down onto the sheets. He sleeps in the fetal position, curled up tight like a little cashew. I lay next to him, with an arm flopped over his body, and let his warm head tuck up against my neck, under my chin, as he'd only allow in sleep.

I fell asleep, myself.

When I woke up an hour or so later, the amazing thing had happened.

He'd flipped over. Flipped around so the little cashew was curled in toward me, face pressed to my collarbone. I could just feel his breath in the fabric there, like a secret whispered through a wall. And when I craned my neck and peeked between us, I found his tiny hand fisting the front of my sweater.

He's never held onto me before. I mean, for all I know he turned around because of a stomach cramp. For all I know he was dreaming of his mother, or about clinging to…to who can guess what. But a part of me wants to believe he knew it was me. Smelled me. Needed me.

Is that crazy? I hope not.

I'd have lay there like that forever, but he had another little spell. Not a bad one, just a minute's soft whimpering, and when he settled next he was facing the other way again, clutching the covers and not me. But that doesn't matter. I know I didn't dream it.

Later today, when the sun's high up and the roads have dried out, I'm going to take him for our first run. Between this teeny miracle and the peace you've brought to my body, I'll be able to run and run and run. No matter that it's been months and I've barely slept.

I'll run for miles and miles and miles.

And then maybe I'll fly. Because I can't remember ever feeling this light before.

8.34am

I'm here, Malcolm—though I did sleep. And I did dream, of us. We were in a park, I think, or maybe just a big field. The sort of place I used to love to go to and just spend hours with some falling-apart book that I probably pinched from a library. There was a lot of long grass, shielding us from view.

Though not just us. I'm pretty sure your boy was there too. Making airplane wings with his arms, like my brother used to do. When I woke up, I was full of this strange sense of peace about it.

And what you described only deepened that feeling. His hand clasping you, how happy it made you, all the progress you're making with him. The lightness all of it gave you—god, I'm glad for that. A small part of me was worried that it would have been too much, or too little, or that my greed is overwhelming.

But that part is getting smaller.

All the worried parts of me are getting smaller. Or is it that my courage is getting bigger? I thought about standing in your kitchen, and the need to just be there was so great it practically blacked out all other considerations. In fact, I actually put on shoes.

Do you know how long it's been since I put on shoes?

So long that I couldn't walk around in them. The best I could manage was a pair of ballerina pumps, and a tentative once around the living room. But after I'd done it I sat down with them still on my feet, and I didn't once get the urge to take them off. To throw them back in the bottom of the wardrobe and never think about them again.

They're mine again, now.

And so is the balcony. I went out on it again today, but not just because of you and all the things I'd like to do. Because I wanted to. That glimpse of the world has made me curious for more, so I crept out just after dawn and watched. A guy at his sink across the street, draining his morning cup of coffee. Three girls laughing and golden and gleaming with glitter, stumbling towards home. Someone setting out a sign for a cafe I've never been to.

Chocolate soup, it said, and that urge was there again.

To go out there and see what chocolate soup actually is.

God, I want to know what things actually are.

P.S. Yes, I have a fringe. Or bangs, as you say.

2.32pm

Rest easy in the knowledge that the world isn't passing you by entirely—I have no clue what chocolate soup is, either. And I'm a recovering hipster.

Part of me wants to order you to walk out your door, down the hall, into the elevator, punch a button labeled L, drop down all those floors and march through the lobby, cross the street, and find out.

But another part says no, let's stay in. I'll cook us soup. Non-chocolate soup.

I know a few recipes. Caldo verde and slow-cooker split pea and this really amazing African stew that's made with sweet potatoes and red beans and peanut butter. I know that last one sounds weird, but it's so fucking good. You squeeze lime juice into it, and it's like sex in your mouth.

I'll find us some really good crusty bread from the bakery, and we'll eat soup like it's been outlawed for indecency.

I ought to admit I'm not myself just now. I'm feeling weirdly manic, actually. Can you tell?

I went for a run, like I said I would. We got rained on a little, but overall it went great. The boy didn't make a peep, and we went over six miles. Too far, really, because now I've got terrible heel blisters from my new sneakers, and I'll probably wake up with shin splints, but I couldn't stop. And I don't care.

I feel that way still. Like I can't stop.

I can't figure out if this is just what feeling good again is like compared to feeling depressed, or if I've swung the other way temporarily. If I really have gone a little manic. It feels as though I've drunk eight espressos and I want to clean everything. Make everything new.

I feel like how my mom used to get, those times when she had a recurrence. Like I want to clean the whole world.

I remember coming downstairs around midnight when I was about twelve, the night after she'd been to the oncologist and gotten bad news. There was a scary noise coming from the basement, and I found her down there in the laundry room, and there were a dozen tennis balls banging around in the dryer. She'd washed them, and she was waiting there with a lint brush for when they were dry.

"It's so nice when they're all fuzzy and bright like new, don't you think?"

She wasn't crazy. Not really. I get it now. Whenever she got bad news about her cancer, she wanted to live live live live live live live. Live times a thousand. She wanted to do everything, taste everything, sing every song, make everything fun.

Make our old tennis balls the color of highlighters again.

I think I'm doing that too, a little bit. Only I didn't get bad news. I'm just feeling alive and awake for the first time in months. I want to run until my feet bleed and polish all the doorknobs.

But more than that, I want to ask about you. May I? You don't have to answer every question. Pick one or two.

Did I get the rest of your hair right? Is it darkish brown, the color of milk chocolate? Is it wavy?

What color are the shoes? Tell me how they felt on your feet. Every little detail of them.

What was your favorite book—or three—when you were a kid? Ones worth stealing from the library so you never had to give them back? Especially as I suspect you were probably a good girl who normally followed all the rules.

What's your brother like? Is he older or younger? Did he watch your back when you were kids or put worms down your shirt? Or both? I bet a brother could be a mix of hero and bully.

I hope you're having a nice day, with a good movie or book lined up for the afternoon.

Do you have Netflix? If so, one of these evenings we'll have to pick something to watch together. At the same time, I mean, like, we both hit play at exactly ten. Maybe something really terrible, so we could text snarky shit to each other through the whole thing.

Okay, I'm off to polish the doorknobs. Not literally. Also not euphemistically. Probably going to clean the fridge, though. Something in there smells like rancid butt.

Later, Maya-stranger. Bug you once the boy's gone to bed. Maybe sooner.

3.22pm

Your mom doesn't sound crazy. She sounds right.

And you sound right too. Vibrant and alive and full of all the best ideas in the world. Elevators and eating stew and staying in and answering questions… They're all things I never knew I wanted so much and yet I do, I do, I do.

So I'll start by offering you all the things you want to know.

Yes, you got my hair right. Darkish brown, wavy. Like it's always left to dry while pressed against a pillow—which it usually has been.

The shoes, the shoes…a deep blue with little bows on. When I started to have some money of my own, they were the first things I bought. And I was so proud of them, so happy to have them. I thought they were the swankiest things in the world. Of course they weren't at all, and they definitely aren't now—they're all scuffed around the edges and worn, like the velveteen rabbit.

But they still felt so good on my feet. Roomy and familiar.

And I was a good girl, oh yes I had to be a good girl for most of my teenage years. It was just that I wanted those books so badly. At night I used to lie there terrified, imagining the police coming to put me in prison for taking them. Yet somehow, even that didn't scare me enough to not do it. In fact, after a while I started to wonder if it would be better if they did.

All the reading I could have done in my cell.

Because no amount of reading was ever enough. I'm not even sure if I can narrow my favourites down…there were so many I loved. Moondial and Behind the Attic Wall and Neverending Story. All those books about American girls getting murdered and making out and going steady. Ah, they drove me wild with envy.

Even the dead ones.

As for what I'm doing now: I'm totally waiting for you to read my hell yes let's watch a movie together that is the greatest suggestion anyone has ever made in the history of mankind. And then we can do that as soon as possible, because it's glorious and magical and right.

All we have to do is decide which one.

8.30pm

Evening, you.

I ate up every detail you shared like…like… Like candy, but I'm trying to figure out which kind.

Some kind that comes in different flavors, and different shapes. So I could turn each one around with my tongue and taste it and feel it and savor it. The only candy coming to mind that meets that description is Runts, though, and Runts aren't that great. Especially not the banana ones.

Maybe there's a better, British candy that fits my simile.

I have to say, though, there was a little grain of sand in my candy box. My tooth came down on it, and I flinched, because you said you'd tell me all the things I wanted to know. You left one question out. I don't know if you did it on purpose, and I'm not in a mood to pry, so I won't.

I can picture your shoes now. I can half-picture you in them. You're like a sketchy watercolor drawing with details penciled in here and there. Your hair, your eyes. Your shoes and your hands.

It's much nicer than if you simply texted me a selfie, some picture posed before a bathroom mirror, phone in hand. I like the mystery of you. The paint-by-numbers.

I never knew The Neverending Story was a book! You must know it's a movie. I think I watched it about twenty times the summer I turned eight or nine. I got it for my birthday and played it until the VCR chewed it up. I can barely remember anything about it now.

Wait a second…

8.40pm

Guess what's on Netflix?! Any interest in that? Or is it one of those childhood movies you'd rather not discover is totally terrible to watch once you're an adult? I rewatched The Wizard a while back and couldn't believe how bad it was, considering how much I loved it as a kid. It was basically a two-hour ad.

But some kids' movies stay great, like The Princess Bride and The Iron Giant, and anything involving Jim Henson. So you never know.

Anyhow, I'd be up for it.

8.57pm

Wine gums, you want wine gums. Do you have wine gums in the US? Some are strawberry and some are lime and then there's this one that doesn't taste like anything that exists. That one's my favourite. I call it the white one, even though it isn't white at all. It's sort of translucent and kind of yellow, and yes I realise I'm talking way too much about wine gums.

I didn't intend to. I want to caps lock you to death about Neverending Story instead. Firstly because you watched it until your VCR chewed it up, which is amazing and stupidly made my heart start beating fast like you'd just declared undying devotion. And then secondly because oh my god let's watch it IMMEDIATELY.

It has to be that. I don't care if it doesn't hold up. I just need to watch it with you, as if we are a completely normal couple slouched together on the couch with our snark radars on red alert.

9.13pm

You, me, Neverending Story. It's a date. Hit play at precisely 10:30? I should be done with my nightly chores by then, and if the boy's going to wake it almost never happens before 2am.

10.29pm

You ready, stranger?

I'm ready!

PLAY!

Holy shit, I remember this music!

Okay, so I had totally forgotten how crazy amazing this song was.

It's like the eighties are assaulting me in the face, and I love it.

That's it. That's exactly it. My ears can barely handle the complete eightiesness they're hearing.

Was he dreaming the credits, or…?

I wouldn't put it past this film. His dreams are very red and like a disco in a working men's club in 1985.

I'm totally taking notes on single fatherhood.

It's like his dad is a science teacher who accidentally walked into the wrong house. Start facing your problems?? I think he's about four years old.

Note to self: tousle the boy's hair.

Sorry, I got very invested then. I had his exact haircut and suspect kids would have put me in a dumpster as a kid, if we had dumpsters here.

Awww.

I'd tousle your hair, too. If you were here.

And tweak my nose?

Only if it's consensual.

Everything is consensual when it comes to you.

Duly noted. Dude, this store is like stranger-danger central.

It's like he's luring him into his gingerbread house, only the house is made of books. Which actually sounds pretty cool, to be fair.

Fewer ants.

Plus, being cooked in an oven would probably be a reasonable price for getting to read something that gives you a dragon that grants wishes. I mean, I would take that if I got the dragon first.

I feel like I know everything I need to know about you from that one text. Also, this room is amazing. Kids' movies always have amazing old dusty secret rooms.

Oh my god, I know. Do you have any idea how jealous I was of these American kids with all their enormous houses and awesome attics that probably had Beetlejuice in them or summat?

This giant… That's how I feel right now, after crippling myself, running all that way. Except I want bourbon instead of rocks.

I dunno—I distinctly remember feeling those rocks looked delicious. Easily better than bourbon. This monster really sold me on them.

Oh god, here he comes. Or wait, never mind. I thought the creepy dragon was coming.

I think we have to get to Atreyu first. Maybe?

BTW I only said maybe there because I completely remember everything now, and I'm trying not to seem like a nerd who watched this film way too much.

You totally have me fooled. I didn't suspect a thing when you (a) remembered his name and (b) knew how to spell it.

shamefaced

Also, the effects are frigging amazing. I know people moan about CGI, but seriously we should moan more. I love the way all of this looks.

I love painted backdrops. Even if you can see the seams.

Oh, and Muppet strings. I love those clear Muppet strings and sticks, like when Kermit is waving his arms around.

The strings and seams only make it sweeter.

So was Atreyu a babe when you were, like, eight?

I think I had a lot of confused feelings about him. At one point, I'm sure I was convinced he was a girl.

That would've been an awesome twist. Like at the end of Metroid.

I think I thought Sebastian was lying or fooled when he said a little boy. Or maybe I just identified a lot with Atreyu. I had Sebastian's hair but looked like Atreyu.

Is it totally cheesy that the horse riding and music gave me chills for a second? I blame nostalgia.

Don't. It's good and right to have all the chills. Look how beautiful and cool all of this is.

I hope the boy turns out as earnest and bookish as the narrator kid… And all I can think now is that Atreyu is secretly a girl.

Head canon.

Oh no, that bit is coming. The terrible bit.

I always used to wonder: why did the horse let sadness overtake him? What was he sad about?

Oh shit, I forgot about this. Add this to the list of movies the boy can't watch until he's, like, twenty. Dead pets are just the worrrrssssttt.

I used to fast forward past it. I couldn't stand it. I still can't stand it.

Go get a snack. I'll watch it for the both of us.

Thank you. Thank you. I realise now why I didn't like it.

Okay, it's over. You may return from the kitchen.

While you were gone, the horse swam away to live forever in a beautiful space meadow. It's the director's cut.

Oh, how lovely that idea is. Like rewriting things that have already happened.

I'm highly gifted at denial. It comes in very useful.

Teach me your ways, sensei. I don't want to get emotional about a film with a giant talking turtle in it.

You'll have to choose between a soft heart and a pickled liver—alcohol definitely helps.

I've never been able to drink. But I've often wondered how much fuzzier it would make things. How much softer the sharp edges would get.

You need to get the dosage right. Too much and you just wind up weeping inconsolably. Or I imagine you would. You don't seem like you'd be an angry drunk. Definitely a sentimental one.

Or maybe a silly drunk.

I wish I had your confidence, there. Silly and sentimental sounds okay.

Sorry, now I feel sort of…I dunno, rude, I guess. To talk like I know you well enough to think you're not capable of anger.

No, my Malcolm. Not rude. Not wrong either, exactly. I've never been an angry person. I just always fear that it's in me somewhere, waiting for alcohol to bring it out.

Do you think you deserve to be angrier than you let yourself be?

Oh shit, there's the dragon. Ignore my prying. It's about to get creepy.

It's okay, you're not prying. I do wish I could let myself be angrier sometimes. But now it's hard to be because Atreyu is making a dragon that looks like a penis moan in ecstasy.

I'll pry again soon. But not tonight.

I'm ready for your prying, when soon comes. After we discuss the wang-like qualities of this dragon that seems to get really stoked over being rubbed.

He's like a downy, scaly, flesh-colored flying puppy-phallus. Shudder. And I don't remember these people at all.

They help Atreyu get past the eye lasers I think. And she's the old witch from Willow.

I can't wait for the lasers. That's the bit I remember best. Probably because: boobs.

Gigantic boobs, if I'm recalling correctly.

Without hyperbole, one of the formative sexual experiences of my young life.

I had a girlfriend who said David Bowie's pants in Labyrinth were that for her.

Oh, here we go. Boobs ahoy!

I think the Bowie thing must have affected all us girls, like a bulging contagion.

"Bulging contagion" made me almost spit out my drink.

I don't think I'd make it past the sphinxes. My heart's a hot mess.

They'd probably zap me from seventeen miles away.

My god, those boobs really are skin mag quality.

Nipples and everything.

Also, you'd totally make it. You're so genuine and sweet. If secretly filthy.

If I would, you would. You might think you aren't those things but that's bollocks.

Don't—I've had just enough to drink now to get all feely. How dare you take advantage?

I'm shamelessly opportunistic when it comes to convincing you that you're a good man, the best of men, my lovely one.

I must be allergic to something. My eyes are all weird and watery.

It's probably just raining on your face.

I've just been cutting onions. I'm making a lasagna for one.

That sounds right. We will go with that.

But it's for you, the lasagna. Because I know you probably had something terrible for dinner.

I was just going to say: plus now I get to eat it instead of the super noodles that are congealing on a plate by the couch.

Oh shit, more boobs.

Sometimes the child actor sounds vaguely English.

I think he might have been. But I have no idea how I know this.

Maybe. American actors always tend to go a little English in fantasy movies. You guys are just more magical-sounding.

Well, the posh Brits are. I sound like I'm about to have sex behind some bins.

Okay, that time I DID spit out some of my drink.

I want to ask where you live as badly as I don't want to. I feel like I'm just not supposed to know. Or like you live in some strange vortex with no postal code.

I live in the North East.

Of Fantasia.

Sassy minx.

I always want to know how you pay for all the stuff you must have shipped to your door. And when you last went to a doctor. And a million other questions that seem somehow better unanswered.

I sell edible rocks to fantasy creatures.

>:-(

I don't remember so much of this part… I wonder how many times I stopped watching after the boobs were over.

You don't remember "Come for me, Gamork"??

No!

God, I must have acted out that moment a million times in my head, only with me in Atreyu's place.

My goodness, the stuff he's saying. This is pretty disturbing for a kids' movie. Those who have no hope are more easily controlled… That hit me right in the guts.

Oh, honey.

All the best kids' movies are scary. Or have scary bits.

That's true. I remember being terrified of a lot of films like this. Terrified, but also preferring their version of these horrid things over the real-life versions. Easier to kill a fantasy wolf than the stuff it represents.

I'm guessing no magic dragons turned up to save you in the nick of time when you were little.

Do they ever?

No, not as far as I can tell. If I'm one for the boy, I showed up pretty fucking late to the party.

You were one for him, believe me.

Maybe. Sometimes I worry the inside of the boy's head looks just like this bit now. All dark, empty space and drifting fragments.

Mine did. Mine does. But less so now. You make me feel like maybe the dragon has come, so I don't know why it couldn't be true for him.

He's still so little. I don't remember anything from when I was his age. So I hope maybe he won't either. I hope he won't remember a time when I wasn't there for him.

He might remember a time before. But he'll remember you coming for him more.

I hope so. But I don't feel very heroic. I feel like I'm just fumbling my way through this shit, trying not to make anything worse.

That's the way actual heroes always feel. They get up to the window and shout out the name, even though they are sure it's probably not the right thing to do.

I hope you're right. Though I don't want to be a hero, really. It's so much harder than owning a liquor store. In case you were trying to choose between the two.

Oops, we missed, like, the entire climax of the movie.

Yeah, but I think we got the point of it.

So, do all the characters remember when the Nothing came through, or did the kid turn back time and hit Undo on all the badness?

I don't like the idea that he just undid all the bad. I mean, I guess I wish I could do that for the boy's head, but I can't, so I'd rather the movie end with everyone moving on with their bad memories but being stronger for it or something.

Is it okay if I do want it undone?

Of course it is. I guess I just want to think there's a way to fix all the cracks, instead of just going back and not dropping the vase. You know?

Oh yes, I know. I do. I like both of those options…but one of them will always be the winner for me.

Can I ask you something?

You can always ask me.

It's more rhetorical than anything, because I'm not stupid. I want to ask if you had a traumatic childhood, but I think I already know the answer. But I don't want to ask what happened to you. That feels like too far. So I don't know what I want to ask. But if you have anything you'd like to say, I'm ready to hear it.

Is it enough to tell you yes? Yes, I had a traumatic childhood. Though traumatic seems like such a grand word for things that felt so…mundane. Mundanely bad. Like you know in movies when Julia Roberts has a violent husband? And yet it seems so glossy still. Everything is glamorous and works out okay. Nothing happens awkwardly or too suddenly, and once the villain is vanquished everyone goes on into a wonderful, amazing new life.

I do know what you mean. I wish things here were like a movie. Like, I show up here and everything's really hard for the first hour of the movie, but then there's some miraculous breakthrough like when Helen says "water" and I've gotten through to the boy and everything's good and the music swells and the credits roll.

But you're right. Reality is very mundane. And very un-glossy.

Yes. Yes yes yes yes. Yes. And you KNOW. You know in the movie that someone is coming to save them. The surety is perfect and absolute, and even if it isn't you can just turn it off before it ever gets to that part. But not here. Here, it's the opposite. You're sure no one's coming, and you can't turn it off.

You don't ever have to tell me about your movie, not unless you decide you want to. But could you tell me how the first one ended? Are you in the sequel yet? It's better, isn't it? Safe, if still mundane?

Oh, my Malcolm. Yes, it's better. It's been getting better in ways I didn't fully realise—like a caterpillar in a cocoon, I think, rather than an agoraphobic hermit who doesn't ever want to face reality. But you've made the second act really something.

God knows I don't want you to feel obligated or like I rely on you, because I don't. But you have, and you still will have no matter what happens from here.

Am I shouting down into your well? That's what you do for me. And now, after this last week or two, I can even see a little blue way up there. A tiny little circle of blue.

You're doing more than shouting. You've reached down and grabbed my hand, and I know I can pull myself up. I just hope I can pull you up from yours, too. Or at least give you something that you can use to do it.

I think I called you my bucket a million years ago.

God, it feels like a million years. But in the best way.

If this was a movie, I'd scale your building and come rappelling through your window and carry you off into the sunset. Which would somehow be spectacularly bright and colorful, even though it's always overcast here. And I'd be taller and more muscly than I am. Probably played by Ryan Gosling or whoever.

But I don't think this is a movie.

No. It's better.

That made me smile. Tell me what it is, then.

Not being afraid for once of what happens when you can't just stop watching altogether.

Is it okay that sometimes I want to fast forward to the later bits? The bits that come after 10pm?

It's okay. I want to fast forward to the part where I actually get to hold you in my arms.

I'm wearing kind of a scratchy sweater. Just so you're warned.

I don't think a sweater made of rusty nails and broken glass would stop me.

You should have been here tonight. Watching that stupid-slash-amazing movie on my couch. Eating around the burned kernels in the bowl of popcorn I made. There were a lot of burned ones. That's one thing I suck at cooking. Which is sad, since it comes in a packet with basically one instruction.

I would eat the burned ones gladly. In fact, I'm starting to feel foolish for not being there with you. Scared still, but foolish.

Shit, sorry. Have to go—I hear the boy moaning. More later.

Goodnight, stranger.

Hope he's okay. Night, my Malcolm.

MONDAY

10.10am

Morning, you.

Sorry about the abrupt exit. It wound up being a long, rough night, though I didn't mind it so much. Sometimes it really wears me down into that place of despair, but not this time. Even after maybe three hours' real sleep, I feel pretty functional. I have you to thank for that, you and our date.

Did you get Man vs. Wild in the UK? It was one of those survival shows, and it followed this dude named Bear around the wilderness while he used his Special Forces training to keep from dying, e.g. by sleeping in a hollowed-out elk, or sometimes a hotel room.

Anyhow, in this show, he's forever talking about morale. Like, at the end of a long, harrowing day, he'll build a fire, or boil some tea out of twigs and pine needles, or eat a grub, or drink a canteen of his own warm pee, and then talk about how much better he feels, how it's boosted his morale. (And also boosted his vitamins, pronounced the wrong-ass British way, like "vittamins.")

I'm not into hot pee-drinking, but the morale thing is definitely true. The circumstances of my long night were no different than those of any other I've endured since I moved here, but following on the heels of our movie date, it was so much easier to bear. Like you make me stronger. Or you make dawn worth waiting for, thinking I might get to read your thoughts, learn a little more about you, maybe make you smile and try to picture exactly that.

You're the twig in my pine needle tea, Maya. You're my steaming elk carcass, sheltering me against the dark and cold.

Sorry. I'm feeling silly this morning. Sleep-deprived and smitten. It's a dangerous combination. I'd better not operate any heavy machinery. I can't, anyhow—I'm basically made of mangled jerky from my hips down, thanks to yesterday's run.

What are you up to? I'm about to drink some coffee and sit in the living room with the boy, watch him stare at the tablet probably, and talk, unacknowledged, in his general direction.

I spoke to my aunt this morning—my mom's sister. We used to be pretty close, and I guess we still are, though she only knew the broad strokes of everything that's been happening, here. I've been avoiding her calls, just because there's so much to say, and so much of it hurts.

To be honest, you know way more about it all than my dad even does, which is partly my fault for not calling much, but also partly his for not really asking or seeming interested. I don't want to say he doesn't care… I know him too well to think about it like that.

Anyhow, this time when my aunt called, I answered my phone. I was feeling stronger than normal, no doubt thanks to you. To us and this little Charlie Brown-looking tree of a friendship that we've managed to plant and sprout together.

I told my aunt everything and did an okay job keeping my shit together. She asked what she could do for the boy. I said we have everything we need. Material stuff, at least. I was sitting on his bed while we talked, and I was looking around, realizing just about everything in his room is from the Time Before, as I think of it. The Time Before I showed up, when his life looked like god knows what. I kept it all, because I figured something should be familiar. Now I think maybe I had that all wrong.

It made me worry what memories are tangled up in his plaid sheets and faux-quilt bedspread and the pictures on his walls, and in his few and largely untouched toys.

I told my aunt maybe I ought to redecorate his room, new covers and pillowcases and pictures, maybe buy some curtains. She got really excited and told me she'd send money, that she wants to be a part of it. I don't really need the money, but I told her sure, if it makes her happy.

Now I'm kind of excited myself, to take the boy to some stores and pick out new bedding, maybe a mobile of the solar system like I had…only without Pluto these days, I assume.

He'll probably be as catatonic as always on the mission, but he'll know we picked this stuff out, that it's new, nothing to do with whatever came before. That whatever memories get woven into it all, they'll be safe ones, if not necessarily joyful. I'll do that tomorrow, maybe, or start on it, at least. If my legs work by then.

Wow, check me out, going on and on, and only halfway through my first cup of coffee. I'll shut up now. What are you up to today? What did you get up to after I disappeared on you?

Tell me everything. Fill my eyes all the way up to the brim with you.

11.42am

First of all, it's not silly. I'd be your hollowed out elk any day, and you should know that by now. Second of all, how dare you disparage the correct way to pronounce vitamins! Third of all, your aunt is a wise woman, and you are amazing. The boy will know that you're doing this for him, and it will matter to him. Fourth of all, anything I do that helps you is awesome, the end. Fifth of all, brace yourself for brim-filling.

Things I did after you disappeared:

1. Fantasised about what being there with you would be like. Mostly it was amazing. Sometimes it was terrifying. I managed to stop short of filming the side of my face while I said words to see if I looked like a normal person.

2. Told myself I would never tell you the above in case it made me sound like a serial killer who doesn't understand how to be human.

3. Tried to get some sleep, but failed completely at it. In fact, I haven't been to sleep at all. Something about our movie night just turned me into a jittery, overjoyed mess. Like I'd drunk ten cups of coffee and then discovered my numbers came up on the lottery.

I don't regret comparing you to winning the lottery.

You make me feel like I've won something all the time.

I got all the way to the elevator before I had to go back.

2.45pm

Be careful with your comparisons—doesn't winning the lottery only ever ruin people's lives? Or maybe it's different in the UK.

The boy is down for a nap. He passed out on the couch, half sitting up, so I'm camped in the chair by the window with my feet up on the sill, listening to the tick of the radiator and the drone of some construction truck or other working down the street.

I wish you could have seen me getting my legs into position. They hurt so much, I had to haul each one up with both hands hammocked under my knee. I don't know how I'll ever get them back down.

I meant to tell you, I started Earthsea yesterday. I'm about halfway through already, at the part where what's her name reveals her powers. Some parts of the story hit a little close to home, but I bet the ending's going to cancel out any anxiety it's giving me.

I hope you'll be around tonight. Or rather, I hope you'll be up for talking more. Letting me maybe ask you some questions. If I came right out and asked, would you tell me anything about your parents, I wonder? Or your brother? Would you tell me where you'd go if you found the nerve to hit the call button and step inside that elevator? (You're beyond amazing, you know, to have made it all the way to the elevator. You blow my mind anew every goddamn day.)

If any of those questions sounds like too much, that's fine. I don't want you to be anything more than what you're ready to be, with me. But I think you know…I think you know I have feelings for you. The kinds of feelings you're not supposed to get for people you've never seen or even really spoken to, not for someone you might never meet. But I have, and they're not going anywhere, so I figure it can't hurt to ask.

We could take it slow. I won't barge in like I did when I asked your name.

You can take your time. You can tell me, not that question, not yet.

Or you can turn yourself inside out and tell me everything. I don't care if it's ugly. There's nothing you can say that'll scare me off.

Know that I'm only asking because I want to know you. I won't even say it's because I want to understand you, because that's too fucking grand and too fucking patronizing. I just want to know. There's so much I'll never know about my own son's past, I guess maybe hearing a few bits and pieces of yours would make me feel less alone.

Anyhow, I'll pester you tonight after ten. Until then, keep practicing your normal human speech mechanics.

P.S. I started writing a song about you. I haven't written a song in probably five years. If I drink enough later, maybe I'll share a few of the corny-ass lyrics.

10.39pm

You don't have to barge in, and you don't have to pester. Truthfully, it's always on the tip of my tongue now. Or at the tip of my fingers, if you want to be more accurate. All of which is weird to me, because I spend so much time pretending it never happened. I press my thumb down on the memory so that it can't get out.

I'm here, stranger. Whatever it is you're holding in, just know it'll find a safe home with me.

Good, because it wants to be out, with you. You make it easier to think about somehow. Like you've created a force field around me, and once things have escaped my fingertips they can't beat their way back in with a hammer.

Or at least, not this time.

What do you mean?

That was what he used, you see—though even now I don't think he meant to. I think it was just in his hand, ready for things like locks that were in the way and windows that wouldn't smash on the first try. Only once he was inside, he realised we were there, so he just smashed us instead.

Though I say us. When I really mean everybody else.

Nothing happened to me, safe in my little attic room that he didn't even know was there. It all happened to them—first to my dad, who surprised him on the stairs. Then to my mum, who went to defend her husband. And then to my brother, my brother, I don't know why he killed my brother.

Oh, honey.

He was just a little thing. He barely came up to my waist. His arms were made of sticks and air, and his hair was so fine you could almost see through it.

I know that boy well.

I know you do. I know. So maybe you can tell me: why did he do it?

The police said he surprised the guy too. That he pounced on him to protect my mum, but I don't know. I don't know. I don't want to know, I think. Because if it's true, if he did, then I have to think about him being so good and so brave and know beyond a shadow of a doubt that I wasn't.

I heard them. I heard him. I heard it all.

But I didn't come down.

Honestly, I think I'm still there.

Still waiting to be as brave as my tiny brother, with my hand clamped over my mouth and my face made sticky and taut with tears. Still wanting to go down but not daring to, never daring to. Why didn't I dare to?

I could have grabbed him before he ran to help our mum. Got us both out of a window and away through the fields behind the house. Or maybe if I had fought, too, the tide would have been turned. The murderer was only young, only slight, and only there to take our things. He wasn't expecting a fight.

It might have been all right if I'd joined the fray.

You were a kid. As helpless as your brother.

And part of me gets that. Most of me knows it's just as likely that he'd have killed me too. Sometimes I even wish that, along with all the others. Like the sweetest fantasy of the three—just to be wherever they are, instead of in this hell.

Though I say hell, I say it, when the truth is…it isn't anymore. It was, it really was for a long time. And it was an impervious sort of thing, too. I had counsellors and therapists and foster parents who tried to crack it, and some of them were even nice. Some of them partly got through.

But nothing has ever made me feel as free of it as you do.

Maya.

Don't, don't, just let me say.

You make me feel like a person, not a thing who had that happen to them.

Not a mess of guilt, not a lonely girl made lonelier by families that were not my own, not someone afraid he'll come back even though I know he can't. I'm just me, with you. The one I should have been if time could be turned back and everything started again. Like you were waiting in the dark of our house with a shotgun in your lap.

Then you just blew it all away.

I wish I had been there. Waiting, protecting you. Same as I wish I'd been there for the boy, through whatever he endured before… Before things that I haven't told you the whole truth about.

This sounds ridiculous, considering how we've never even met, never even heard each other's voices. But if I could get in a time machine and be there in that house, with that shotgun laid across my thighs, I would have killed for you. Not happily, but easily. Thoughtlessly.

I'm glad you shared all that. Honored you did, and humbled that you trusted me with it. I'm so, so sorry you went through that.

You don't have to be sorry. I'm not anymore. I'm not even upset, the way I usually get.

That's good, though in all honesty, I'm sobbing right now. My vision's blurred, the words on my screen running like rain on a windshield.

Thank you. I want to know you, the real you. I think you believe that now. You must, to turn yourself inside out like you just did.

I do I did I am. It was so much easier than I ever thought it could be, too.

The strange thing is, I don't feel any different. I mean, I knew there must be something sad in your past, something traumatic. And knowing now what that thing is, and who you lost, and how… It means a lot. But it doesn't change anything about how I feel for you. You're the same person to me. It's like…

It's like, you're a tree.

Bear with me, this is going to be a cheesy analogy, because I'm weepy and I'm just a little drunk.

I'm bearing, in the best kind of way.

But it's like you're a tree, and after just these couple weeks, I know that tree like I've spent my entire life sitting under it. I know which directions the biggest limbs stretch. I know how the leaves ripple and the branches sway in a storm.

Before today, I knew where the knots were, and I knew that someone, at some point, sawed away a limb or two, leaving hard and secret scars, and soft pulpy bits, weeping sap. I knew the tree, and I knew it cast a long shadow. Now, I know what's hiding in that shadow. I know a little about which limb got hacked off and who by. But it doesn't change the tree as I know it.

It doesn't change how I feel. And I feel a lot. More than I dare spell out for you. At least not before another glass of this whiskey.

I'm not even sure if it feels like something daring for me now. I've shared the scariest thing, and you still see the tree that is me. And I promise, I will always see the tree that is you. No matter what you say.

You asked me, way back when we first started texting, whose number yours used to be. Who I'd thought I was texting. I'll tell you now, if you want to hear. If you're not too raw from everything you just shared with me.

There's nothing that could make me not want to.

Your number used to belong to an ex-lover of mine.

I met her over three years ago, when I was in Birmingham for a wine and spirits expo. She wasn't with the convention. We met in a bar, hooked up for a few nights. I didn't even know her last name at the time, and I don't think she knew mine.

She was this beautiful, wild tornado of a girl, all art and music and light and energy. When I was with her, it felt like I was vibrating, so hard my bones might rattle apart. It was exhilarating. And after three nights, exhausting.

I figured she'd just be a fond memory, a merit badge on my Narcissist Scout's sash, proving I was charming and worldly enough to get taken home by a hot English girl.

Then in the spring of last year, I heard from her out of the blue. She'd kept my number. And a year and a half earlier, she'd given birth to my son.

I sent her money. Every month, and didn't ask for proof he was mine. I waited for her to invite me to see him, all the while praying she wouldn't, because I'm a coward. She never did.

Last September, I got another call, this one from her mother. The girl had killed herself, cut her wrist in the bathtub. The police think she tried to drown the boy at the same time but didn't manage it. Only he knows for sure, and he's not talking.

So to answer your question from all that time ago, I didn't think you were anyone. I thought that number belonged to a dead woman, to a SIM card trapped in a forgotten phone, its battery dead, lost in a landfill or an evidence bag or who knows where.

You can understand why I never expected to hear back.

Oh, Malcolm.

I thought she was a free spirit. You know that term—manic pixie dream girl? I guess that only works in the movies. In real life, it's called schizoaffective disorder, and the suicide rate is something like ten percent. Probably higher if you mix in the stresses of single motherhood and a side of drug abuse.

I remember you saying something about a package. About venturing out into your hallway to retrieve a package, seven months ago, I think you said.

It'd be so eerie if that package was a new phone, with a new number. Your new number. Her old one. I've never been able to shake that possibility, not since you first mentioned it.

I think you can't shake it because this feels like something big and crazy and unreal. Like when people talk about fate in the movies, and things come together in a way they never do in reality.

But it is coming together, whether it was a phone or not.

Right? Or am I just dreaming it all?

No, you're not. And here we are, stranger. No more secrets.

I won't lie, yours were hard to hear. It all echoed so loudly what the boy's been through. Or the worst of what I imagine, anyhow.

It feels like we're standing here, naked, with a hundred ugly scars, dark and shining between the two of us.

But…

Forgive me, I'm properly drunk now.

You're forgiven. Always.

But those scars don't scare me. And standing naked here before you, seeing you exactly as you are, it doesn't change a thing. I still want to take you to bed, as badly as I ever had. Worse.

What that says about me… Something noble or something depraved? I can't say.

Can it be both? Though if I have to pick one, is it bad if I say depraved, here? It feels bad. But still, I don't care.

This is going to sound corny as fuck, but even bad stuff feels nice with you. Even when we share really fucked-up memories and feelings, I feel better after. Lighter. Like some kind of psychic blood-letting.

Wow, I'm really drunk.

That doesn't sound corny to me. It sounds right. It sounds perfect. It sounds like all the things I want to say, only they're coming from you. And I can't tell you how much of a relief that is. To have someone say things first.

Can I tell you about something that happened this evening? Something kind of amazing?

Do you even need to ask? I'm already greedy for it before you've even begun. Tell me your something.

Tonight, after dinner, everything was just the usual routine around here. I gave the boy the tablet and plunked him on the couch to swipe swipe swipe while I did the dishes. But when I finished stacking everything in the drying rack and went into the living room, he was gone.

I was scared for, like, ten seconds, because he's the most habitual creature of habit you ever met. It was like I'd misplaced the ceiling or the walls, it was so weird. But I ran around and I found him in my bedroom. He was standing beside my bed. My guitar was lying on the end, and he was just standing there, strumming the strings, so quiet I almost couldn't make it out.

I didn't say anything for a whole minute or more—I didn't want him to stop. But eventually I walked over and stood beside him. I told him, "That sounds really good, buddy."

He didn't look up at me. He never looks me in the eye. But he looked sort of at my feet, and he slid the guitar toward me an inch or two. So I sat down, and I played a few bars, and he just stood there. It was…

It was the best fucking thing.

Of course it was the best fucking thing—he wanted you to play! That's what happened, right? He was asking you to play. Oh, I'm so happy for you, Malcolm. I'm so happy for you both. He knows you and sees you, and you know and see him.

He's in bed now. I wish you were here. What I played for him… It was some of that song I started writing for you. It's almost done. You want to hear a couple lines?

I wish I was there too. But only because I want more than a couple of lines. I want them all, every one. I want to hear every bit of it. Two would be a good start, though.

How about the first verse, then?

You found me, stranger, way down deep in this place /
A man with no name, no voice, no face /
I was counting on silence, but you sent me words /
A girl with eyes like stones, hands like birds /
Eyes I'll never see and hands I'll never feel /
How do you do it, honey? Seem this real?

Is it possible to swoon while still staying conscious? I think at the very least I need a fainting couch. Honestly, what are you trying to do to me?

Speaking of couches, where are you? I'm in the chair by the window again. But if you were here, we could move to the couch. It's rainy and clammy here. Probably the same where you are. The radiator's cranked, but since some genius parked it directly under a single-pane window, it doesn't do much. But we could get under a blanket.

Forget the blanket. Just imagine me tunneled underneath the jumper you're probably not wearing. I'm somewhere around your left armpit, still recovering from the Song of Complete Swoonation. And so cosy I could probably live right here forever.

I am wearing a sweater, actually. And since I'm teasing you, it IS very cozy with a Z.

You can have it. I want all four of our arms free. I want us to dissolve into a big, sloppy octopus of cuddles on this couch. So you take the sweater. I've got a thermal on anyhow.

For a second, I thought the Z was for extra sexiness somehow. And then I remembered I'm just super British and you're just super American. I'm not disappointed though—the thermal upped the steam levels by at least fifty percent.

Are those levels in Celsius or Fahrenheit? I need to know so I don't crank them to 85, thinking that's a bit humid but actually I've boiled us alive.

And the Z was because, bless you, you just don't talk American right. It's not your fault. You're not a cultured people, you English. Plus extra-sexy cozy is spelled COXXXY.

Thank god you got the temperature right. I don't think I could hit you with a teabag while being boiled. That's the correct attack for a Brit, right? Teabag assault?

Or am I supposed to do it with a can of baked beans?

Either way, I'm very ferocious. You're probably lucky you didn't go with coxxxy.

What movie are we pretending to watch on this couch? Tell me while I kiss your neck.

Something sexy. Preferably with all the things I want to do to you in it, so I can segue artfully into all of them. "I've always wanted to do that," I could say, in a completely innocent tone of voice. And then hopefully you oblige.

There's no movie with all the things I want to do with you. There's no movie that filthy and sweet and hot and romantic and cuss-riddled, at least not with the right lighting, the right soundtrack. So let's just say we're

watching Blade Runner because it doesn't really matter—
neither of us is going to remember a second of it.

*I guess we'll just have to make up our own, then. No artful,
innocent segues. No suggestions. Just me telling you what I
want and you telling me what you want.*

There's a thousand things I'm nearly literally dying to know
about you. Like how you taste and how you smell, what
your hands feel like on me. But even more than that, what I
really want to know is how it would go if we were actually
together right now.

Like, you're... What's the right word?

"Innocent" makes me feel creepy.

"Inexperienced" sounds weird too.

You're... Fuck, I dunno. You are how you are. What I
want to find out is, would you want me to lead? Need me
to? Would you ask me to? Ask me to do everything to you
first. I would. You have to know that by now. But I know
things about you, too. And those things make me wonder
just how long I'd lead for. Before you stole those reins and
made a messy, grasping experiment of me.

You don't have to wonder. I think I'm already holding them. At the very least, I don't mind saying that I want to push you back on that couch and lick you from the insides of your thighs to the slant of your jaw. I want to map out your body in bites—never quite going over into painful, but never quite giving you anything sweet, either.

And then when I'm done, I want to begin all over again.

Here's what I want, then. I want your hand at my neck. Your thumb pressed hard to that little hollow behind my ear, tight, so you feel my pulse thumping there. I want those teeth on my other ear, just like you said—almost too hard. And I want that free hand wherever it wants to be. My chest, or under the hem of my shirt. Fingers wrapped around my belt buckle. Anyplace that's almost there, almost there but not quite. And just hear me panting. Because I am.

I can practically feel that pulse through my phone. I can taste your skin. And that coolness against my fingertips is definitely your belt buckle. Now the only question is: how long do I take to give you what you're panting for? A minute? Longer? I think it's going to be longer. There's so much more I want to do before I get to the main event.

I couldn't tell you if it takes a minute or ten years—it'd feel the same, either way. Like an eternity. And I couldn't even tell you what it is I want, aside from pleasing you. Teaching you, letting you explore me. But let me think.

I want your voice, I know that much. I don't even know what it sounds like, but I want your voice, right there against my neck. Words, or just your breathing, or sounds. I couldn't guess what you'd give me, only that it would drive me wild.

At this point, it would have to be all three. Me telling you things like give it to me, even though I barely know what I want you to give. Maybe some sounds every time I taste some new part of you, or hear you respond to whatever I'm doing. Because that's what would get me: knowing how this was making you feel. God, I long to know exactly how this is making you feel.

It's making me feel like I'm slowly melting and maybe exploding at the same time. My skin is practically vibrating, and so far I haven't even taken off your pants.

Fuck, I need you in my bed.

I'd knock that hand off my belt buckle and grab you by the wrist, all but dragging you past the kitchen and down the hall, into my room. It's dark. I slam the door behind us.

You probably can't make out much of anything aside from the gap in the curtains, the slice of streetlight there. But you'd feel my messy covers as I lay you down across my bed. Cool cotton, almost cold—this room's always cold. But then me, above you, burning alive.

I see it all—the room, the light, you. And I feel you. I feel that urgency in the way you grab me and drag me and lay me down. In the way you slam that door. It takes me higher than I've been before. It makes me react in kind: almost wildly, I think. Bucking up against you before you've done a thing. Begging for more instead of being patient.

I can't be patient with you. I don't want to be anymore. I want you bare, and my greedy, grasping hands are there to make that happen. They're wrenching at whatever clothes you might be wearing, too desperate suddenly to stop.

Please tell me you don't want me to stop.

I don't, no. I've never wanted anything worse than I want this. But the thought of your hands, grasping at my sweater and my jeans… That changed things. That made me want to slow this all down. To imagine this is us, for real. Together, in the same dark room… I want to tell you stop, just for a minute. Slow down. I want to switch on the light so I can see you. I don't want to miss an inch of your skin or a single expression passing across your face.

Lie down with me, on our sides. Let me kiss you for an hour, until you've learned everything that people spend high school figuring out, one awkward teenage kiss at a time. Just feel what I do, try to do the same back. Would you like that?

Now I'm blushing over the thought of my clumsy rushing—but even that has a sweetness to it. It feels good to stumble and crash headlong into things, and then have you catch me, guide me, show me how this should go. Is that crazy? It feels a little crazy, but I don't care.

Because you wanting to see me makes me crazier. And the thought of getting those awkward teenage kisses—yeah, that's even better. I think of you saying part your lips for me or put your hand in my hair, and I go ever so slightly out of my mind.

Though I don't quite know why. I just know that I'm a seething mess, long before the hour of kissing is up. By the third touch of your lips I'm probably pleading with you for more, body bucking on the bed, always trying to go a little too far. Can you see me like that? Can you see how I really am right now?

I'm smiling. It made me smile to think of you bucking and squirming with impatience, so I'll take pity on you—no full hour of kissing.

I want to rush too, trust me. But if this were reality... It wouldn't be like these texts. I couldn't go back the next day, relive each and every thing that was said and done with perfect recall. And I don't want to miss anything. So I suppose that's how we'd be, stranger—you rushing, me slowing you. I find that quite charming, actually.

Now tell me this—when I undress you, are you shy? Or do you not even bat an eye?

I think it would have to be both at the same time. Thinking about what you would think of me would make me want to stop you. Especially if you did it the way I think you would. Slowly, I bet. Peeling off one piece at a time. Maybe savouring every step, because you're right. That's you.

Guilty.

And I'm the one who wants to rush. I'm the one who's been starved all these years; I'm the one who feels impatience so deeply it's like being dominated by it. It overrides everything else—a thirst that I can't check or satisfy.

It would definitely get the better of any shyness, eventually. I know it would, because it's getting the better of me now. It makes me want to tell you things I shouldn't: like what you'd find as you took off each item of clothing.

So tell me.

The flush all over every inch of me, the stiffness of my nipples, the roll of my hips and the wetness between my legs. It's all there, just waiting for you to uncover. And I want you to uncover it, I do. Never doubt that.

Fuck.

Now it's me who's wanting to rush. But I won't. Because you're right, you know me well enough after even this short time.

I have brown eyes. I don't know if I ever even mentioned that before, but I do. I have brown eyes, and they make an inventory of you, every new sliver of pale skin I uncover as I undress you. That much I'll take slow. I don't ever want to forget this moment, the first time I get to see your naked body.

But what you said, and what I'll find—you, wet. That changes everything. All my best romantic intentions to take this at a glacial pace, it all falls apart at that little word. My cock's aching, here in reality, and there in that room we've created together. And it's not cold anymore. All I want is to get inside you, so bad it's like I'm dying every second it'll take to get there.

I'm dying just seeing you say that. Thinking of the way I look between my legs—slick, so slick—being the thing that pushes against your control. Your need to take things slow. And imagining what you look like now, as you imagine me like this.

Are you still inside your jeans, pressing against the material all thick and heavy? I think so. I think you're straining in a way that makes me want to grab, to unzip, to map things out greedily with my hands.

But you've already held me back twice. You've pressed the need for patience into me, and that stops me short.

Do you still want me to stop short?

Fuck no. And fuck patience.

I was wrong. All we've ever had were words. Words and nothing but words. So the first time we ever touch and kiss and lay our eyes and hands on each other, let it be your way. There's no other way it could be. Fuck words.

Also, fuck my clothes. Fuck this sweater. I peel it away along with the shirt beneath it, fling them to the floor. Your curious hands—fuck those too, if only for the moment, because I need to get these pants off before they strangle me.

There's a clatter as my belt hits the floorboards, a rustle as my jeans join the heap, but no words. Just my shorts now, and I grab your hand and put it right where I need it, curl your soft palm around my hard cock. Hold it there, just for a breath. Then I'll show you how to touch me, with slow, tight strokes through the cotton.

And no words. Just breathing. Just my moans as I let your hand go, let you take over.

Yes, god yes, let me take over. Let me be clumsy and too eager and out of control. Guide me, and then let me go. I can go. I know what feels good—I can tell by the look of you, the sound of you. We don't need words anymore, you're right. This is enough. Just my hand on your cock, stroking greedily. And you knelt over me, urging me on with every sigh and groan.

Oh, just the thought of you sighing and groaning. Just the idea of your cock in my hand, straining against my grip.

I'd have to put a hand between my own legs as I worked you. Is it okay to put a hand between my own legs as I work you? I hope so, because it's happening. It's there in this fantasy, and it's here in reality, and oh it feels so good I don't know if I can stop—not even if you want me to.

I don't. You keep doing that, and I'll tell you what happens next.

I'm kneeling above you. I'm torn—my eyes want to see it all, every stroke you give me, but it's so good. Too good.

My eyes shut and my head cocks back, my mouth's open and I'm panting, helpless.

But it changes, in time. There's aggression now, that almost angry feeling when you want somebody this bad, need them this bad. I'm meeting your pulls with my hips, thrusting into your fist. And soon that's not enough either. I know how it must feel between your legs. What you're feeling now, against your fingers. And I want that so fucking much. It'd be so easy to peel your fingers from me, shove your legs wide with mine, pin your hands to your sides and take exactly what I want from you.

But I won't. Not without asking, because there's no way I'm fucking that bit up, even if I know you're screaming for this, too. So fuck words, still, but I'd have to utter these four, before we go any further—

Do you want me?

I'd say here that you don't need to ask, but that would be a lie.

Because asking makes me so wild I barely know what to do with myself. I'll think of those words every time I touch myself from here to eternity. Just knowing you want to take me, but stop to ask. That you broke the heavy silence to get those words out.

And I'd say yes. You know I'd say yes, right?

Take what you want. Take it now.

I wish I knew what this moment feels like for a woman. I don't.

I can only tell you how it would feel to me. How hot your skin would be as I held my cock, drew my head up and down your lips. Nothing's ever felt so slick, and soft, and lush. It's my last shred of self-control, taking those few seconds, those few strokes.

But the time for control's over now. I'd angle myself, find that spot. You'd welcome me in, but I wouldn't sink deep—not at first. You're too flushed, too tight. I know it's from wanting me. I know it's the answer to that question I just asked you.

So I don't slip inside. I push, just softly, just enough. There you are. You're hot like a fire, deep and dark, swallowing me whole, and so much more than my cock, it seems. I wish I could tell you how it would feel for you. Perhaps your fingers inside you could give you some idea. Are you there already? Imagining it's me?

You know I am. I was there before I even told you to take me. I was there as soon as you started talking about my hand around your cock. Two fingers sliding inside my pussy—which is as swollen and tight and slick as you described. It's so slippery I can hardly do this with any skill. But I'm trying, because I want that echo of you. That idea of you pushing into me, slowly like you said. That sense of being spread and filled.

Because that's what it's like. Even when it's just me, easing my thin little fingers back and forth—that's what it's like. My body welcomes the intrusion and clings to it when I draw back. And every now and then, when I hit that spot inside me just right, when I fuck into myself hard enough and can picture you perfectly, can feel the fantasy of your cock just right, I tighten around whatever is thrusting into me.

I tighten and roll my hips right into it. Seeking more. Needing more. Moaning for more. God, can you hear me moaning for more?

I can.

And I'm fucking you now—there's no other word for it.

Can you touch yourself while I fuck you? Say yes, please say yes, because I won't last long, not tonight. Not the first night with you, Maya. Touch yourself, because you know how, exactly. I'll learn how too, soon. So soon, but tonight I'm a wreck, and it's all because of you. Help me get you there before I lose myself. Put your free hand on my hip and show me how fast you want me, how rough.

Here in my room, alone, with just your words, I'm close too. My belt's undone, and my fly's spread open, my cock's out and hard and heavy and hurting, but I barely dare touch myself, as I read your thoughts. Tell me you're close and I will. Tell me when you get there and I'll be right behind you. It'll take nothing at all, I'm so lost in you. In your body, inside my head. You're everywhere. Now help me get you where you need to be.

Oh baby, I'm already where I need to be. My fingers are on my clit as you fuck me, but it's not that frantic rubbing and stroking that really gets me there. You have to know that's not what gets me there. It's the idea of you losing it. Of you holding back for me. I can practically see you above me, trembling with the need to just come and come and come.

But you don't need to wait. Don't wait, because I'm right there. My clit is swelling against my busy fingers, and my body is just one big shuddering mess. And you should hear me—god, I'd love you to hear me. I'd love to hear you.

Do you moan when you come? Tell me. Tell me as I do it.

Fuck, I'm so fucking close. Moan's not the right word. It's a sound. Like seething. A desperate sound sucked through my teeth. Honey, it hurts. Make it stop hurting. Just tell me where—tell me where to come and I will. So goddamn hard.

Inside me. Come inside me—fuck yes, that's what I want. Fill me, fill me as I go over yes now now now. Now, Malcolm.

11.59pm

Are you there? Maya?

I'm still here. Just.

Me too. In a sweaty, undignified heap with my pants still half off, but I'm here.

I look like I've been destroyed by a sex hurricane. Somehow my underwear is on the dressing table—though I don't remember hurling it. Maybe the ghost of you did it.

Never stop looking exactly like that.

Fuck.

Sorry, I swear so much. Though it's your fault, really. But FUCK.

I love your swearing. I want to marry your swearing. Your swearing and me are going to run away together to a fantasy world.

You and your fantasy worlds.

There's so much I want to teach you about sex. Real sex—not just the hot things. Like, I want to show you how some of the sexy shit people get up to in movies is so fucking stupid. Like how fucking in the shower is completely impossible, not unless you enjoy slipping and hitting your head on the edge of the tub, or taking turns being the one scalded by the tap or standing there on the other end all wet and shivering.

And how anything involving food is the fucking worst. Like how you'll have to sleep on your bare mattress that night if you don't want to lay on a souring, sticky puddle of whipped cream.

That's the shit that pops into my head sometimes when we talk, all this ridiculous, anti-sexy stuff, but it feels so intimate to me. All the stuff that fails. Maybe because it'd be so easy just to keep on saying only the cinematic stuff. Easy and obvious.

Do you honestly think that's anti-sexy? To share things like that with me? I live in fantasy. That's all I have. So far, fantasy is really all we've had. And it's lovely and awesome and safe—it's made me feel very safe. But it's done the opposite of what reality usually does. I imagine it dampens things for most people.

For me, it's a raw and ridiculous thrill. I'm almost craving those mistakes. The frantic fumblings and fucked-up things we could dream up together. And I shiver over you saying them all to me, telling me how it would really be.

So go on, go on. Share with me how it really feels.

Tonight, everything we did, everything we said… It was perfect, worthy of that movie that doesn't exist. But if it were all real, if you and I were actually real…

Maybe three days from now, I'm going to go down on you for forty-five minutes, until my jaw's aching and my left arm's gone numb. You're going to start panicking because you haven't come yet. Then you'll get close, so close, only you'll get a charley horse right before you get there, and you'll just about fall off the bed, it hurts so bad.

Three weeks from now, we'll be fucking for ages. You've come already, maybe twice, three times. And now it's me who's close. But I really, really need to pee. But I'm so close, and so stubborn. But eventually I'll shout, "Fuck!" and I'll limp out of the room to piss so I can fucking finish already, because that's how sex looks, sometimes.

Three months from now, one of us will fart in the middle of it all, and we'll die a little inside and pretend like it didn't happen.

Three years from now, we'll fart in the middle of it and not think twice. And I can't fucking wait, because I've never gotten there with anyone. I've never been that comfortable. But I know I could be, with you.

I never thought I'd say that not thinking about farts sounds like heaven, but it does. All of that does. You make even my silliest fears seem like sexy things I should want.

I want those years with you. Those messy, so real years.

If we were together for real…you and me, on that couch the way we started tonight…

As much as I'd want to race to all the predictable places, I almost want to take those hands, move them away. I want to fall back and drag you down with me, just feel the weight of you on top of me, wrap my arms around you and sigh or laugh or fucking cry, I couldn't even guess which. I want to ignore my dick and just let that impatience simmer inside me. Listen to you breathing, listen to whatever's happening at this point in Blade Runner, and when the DVD ends, listen to the radiator ticking and the rain hitting the window.

That doesn't seem strange to me. It seems lovely—just to lie there with you, maybe feel your heart beating against the side of my face and smell whatever you smell like and know that you want it, you want me, but at the same time that you need something else too. I'm the one who was racing ahead to sex. You're the one who wants to slow down and savour.

I can't deny there's something sweet about that.

Fuck, Maya…

There's something I want to say to you.

But I can't. Not quite.

Because I'm not drunk enough.

And because I'm too drunk.

Because to say it now would be a waste. Because I'd wake in the morning and remember, and I'd know I said it at the wrong time, and be sad I was too buzzed to trust that I could remember it right.

But I think you know what I mean. I don't know if you want to hear that, to read that. Not yet, or ever. I don't know. I hope maybe you do. I hope maybe my saying what I am, it's like that hand on my buckle, the way we started out. So close, too much, yet not anywhere near enough. Maybe it'll simmer inside you, sweet torture. Maybe I'd make you wait.

Maybe I'd make you wait, because I could only ever say it in person.

You don't have to do anything but say it in person, if that's what you need. I'm okay to wait, or to only go the places you feel comfortable going. After all, you wait for me. I'm the reason you can't say it in person, yet you don't make me feel bad about it. So in this, I won't rush you. Tell me what you want, when you want to.

I can tell you one thing right now. I can tell you how we'd fall asleep if you were here. Us, realizing once again how cold this room is, with our sweat cooling. I'd want us to take our clumsy turns using the bathroom, feeling awkward and shy, realizing how we're naked, how we managed to forget about it during the sex. I'd want you in one of my shirts and nothing else. Watching you leave my room, watching you come back, your breath smelling like my toothpaste and the rest of you smelling like sex. I'd try to make the covers warm. Your feet would be ice blocks, but I'd just hold you closer, tucking your head and your messy sex hair under my chin, hugging you from behind.

God, you give good reality. Yes to all of that. Yes to your shirt, yes to the taste of your toothpaste, yes to me curling into the curve of your big body. I'd be your little spoon, so comfortable that I think I'd almost be unconscious before I'd had a chance to say goodnight.

I'm yawning. Maybe you can even feel it against the crown of your head, smell that same toothpaste. Should we say goodnight, right here? Both of us in my bed, before the orgasms burn off and the imagining gets harder?

That sounds sweet to me, I have to say.

Perhaps tomorrow night, I'll take your virginity all over again.

Picture me laughing as I drift off to sleep.

I can feel you here in my arms, trust me.

All right, someone has to say it first. Goodnight, Maya.

Goodnight, Malcolm. Sweet dreams.

TUESDAY

6.43am

It's just starting to get light here, and I haven't slept a wink. Instead I've just laid awake, as sweetly tortured as you wanted me to be. Imagining what you wanted to say; knowing what it was anyway.

And cursing myself for focussing on your reticence instead of wondering if you were really asking me to say yes. Yes, I want to hear you say it. Yes, I wanted to read the words. I'm not afraid of them, or of you letting me down when I do.

In fact, I'm not even afraid of saying them myself. Of taking that leap over the chasm of what-if-he-doesn't and braving the swamp of I'm-so-sure-he-won't. And once I'm on the other side, I'll show you the way:

I love you, Malcolm. I love you.

4.17pm

Was it not enough to help you across?

Because I can do better:

I love you like cheese toasties and my blue shoes and the ending of Neverending Story. I love you the way I used to love being alone. My love is a bridge—and not the scary kind from Indiana Jones. The strong kind, like that one people have to paint continuously because it's so enormous.

You're safe to join me on the other side, I swear.

Nothing has to be different once you get there.

WEDNESDAY

5.27am

Okay, I don't want to be worried.

But I'm now genuinely worried that I've said the wrong thing.

And if I have said the wrong thing, then you should really know: we can pretend I never said it at all. Just rewind and go back to whatever it was you were actually going to say, and then I'll answer that instead.

I don't want to push you, because you've never pushed me.

THURSDAY

1.34am

Are you there?

Malcolm. Are you there, still?

Please just tell me you're there, because part of me is honestly starting to wonder if I just imagined you somehow. Like maybe I'm sleeping while Tyler Durden texts me from a secret phone I don't know I have.

Or I guess it could be that you were a ghost.

I have a lot of them. They're bound to attract more.

Just a couple of words would really reassure me that I haven't attracted more.

FRIDAY

10.00am

You don't have to be with me again.

There's no need to say anything sweet.

But if you could just message me that you're not dead. That you haven't died, somehow, that you're not gone. I can't stop thinking that you might be gone. I mean, that's been a pretty strong theme in my life. People I love are there, and then suddenly they're gone.

And I don't mind, I wouldn't mind, if you were only gone because you realised this was too much or too foolish or too something. I can carry on okay if I'm just foolish.

But I don't know if I can carry on not knowing if something happened to you.

Please, at least give me that.

SUNDAY

12.01am

Goodbye, my love.

MONDAY

Unknown Number

6.17pm

Are you there, stranger?

I'm here. Mostly. A bit misshapen.

I've got so much to catch you up on. When did we last talk?
Almost a week ago, I think. It must have been, since it was
Tuesday morning when I got partially run over by a
hatchback.

We said a lot of things that night, and one of us wasn't entirely sober. I hope you didn't think I was ghosting you. It's been torture, not having any way to get in touch.

Let me back up.

So. Tuesday morning I took the boy out for a run. I'd had big plans for the afternoon, to go on our first mission in search of bedding and all that stuff I'd mentioned. I think we were probably three miles in when... Well, I don't remember the moment it happened. But basically a car shot out of a blind drive and hit us.

The boy's fine. I want to throw up when I imagine what would've happened if I'd been running just a tiny bit slower, the stroller taking the hit instead of me. But he was okay. The stroller got flipped into the road, I was told, but for that price you better believe it was safe, plus the street was quiet. He had a couple scrapes on his face, but they're already faded almost to nothing.

Me, I'm not quite so lucky.

I've got a shit ton of bruises and a broken collarbone and my arm isn't so much fractured as... Crushed? I won't get graphic, but suffice it to say it was disgusting, and it's going to take months to heal and it might not ever work quite right again. But on the plus side, it's my left arm and I'm right-handed.

I'm texting very slowly now, let's say.

What else? The woman who hit me... Not even a woman. A girl. I was really, really angry at first, right up until she came to see me the day after the accident. She's seventeen, and I swear she was more traumatized than me about almost killing some dad and his little boy. She was a fucking wreck, probably needs therapy for a year. So my anger's fallen aside, for the most part.

One thing that's come out of this whole nightmare that's sort of miraculous was how the boy reacted. Like I said, I don't remember what happened right when I got hit. I think I came out of shock a few minutes later. By then, someone had gotten the boy out of the stroller. The first thing I was aware of besides the pain was that he was on me. Like, physically on me, latched to my leg and shrieking "Da! Da! Da!" over and over. Which, as it turns out, is his first word.

So that was actually rather special, in its perverse way. Not how I'd have chosen to snap the kid out of his selective muteness, but here we are.

Since the accident, he's also said "tar" and "mag jee," which mean guitar and mac and cheese, respectively.

What else?

Oh! I was on the local news. They interviewed me on Wednesday in the hospital. The accident was the most interesting thing that's happened around here in ages, apparently. If you ever wanted to know what the boy and I look like, you could probably Google your way there.

And that's the gist. I'm not sure what became of my phone, whether it got run over or lost or picked up by somebody after I got taken off to A and E.

The boy's grandma got me a temporary one from a corner store. But I didn't have your number, and I'd never logged into my O2 account for any reason, just paid the paper bill and tossed the records. So I had no idea what my account info was or if I had a password, didn't even know my own fucking phone number. And I was stuck in the hospital for days. I got home last night, and today my only mission was to get to the nearest O2 shop and convince somebody to print me out a copy of my latest statement. Which is how I have your number!

I have no idea what you may have been texting me since we last spoke. That's all trapped on my missing SIM card, along with all of our other texts.

That's been the worst loss, in a way. Losing our history.

We have a history, one that's been entirely documented. The moment we met, the moment we first went to bed together in our weird way. The moments we turned ourselves inside out and bared everything, and the moment I nearly said something to you, something I now wish I had.

I have no idea if you've been angry or sad or scared all this time I've been silent, though I can safely assume you were confused. Maybe pissed. Maybe you blocked my number. If so, guess I got around that one!

I know I'm coming off kind of weird and up and cheerful. Part of that's the pain pills, but part of it's because I'm pretty fucking lost, and when I feel lost I tend to act like everything's extra fine.

But things aren't fine.

I hurt. All the time. Down an arm and a collarbone, I'm basically useless, especially when it comes to caring for a toddler. The boy's grandma is here a lot, and I appreciate that, but I don't enjoy it.

I can't really bathe; I've got a massive cast, and I can't even wrap it in trash bags or whatever, because that requires the use of both hands. Sponge baths—hooray.

Even texting hurts. I have to tap the screen just so, otherwise it tweaks a tendon or nerve all the way up my good arm and tugs at something painful in my busted collarbone.

I can barely get food out of packages and into either of our mouths, to say nothing of cooking. And I probably don't need to spell out the guitar situation.

His grandma's been staying with us while I adjust. I'm basically a stinky, ungroomed, doped-up misery, pretending to feel warm and grateful toward a woman I frankly don't like especially.

My aunt's offered to come and help, but she can't get over here until early April. And even then, she can't stay for more than a couple weeks.

It's looking like I'm going to have to head back to the States.

7.26pm

Had to just pause and stare at those words for a few minutes.

I've given it a lot of thought. What's best for the boy, and what it is I want, myself. I think it makes the most sense. If I go back, my aunt can help long-term, part-time, instead of just for a couple weeks around the clock. I mean, I couldn't afford a visiting nurse here for long.

It'll take some time to move. Not stuff-wise—I hardly brought anything over, and the flat came furnished, so it'd just be my clothes and the boy's things, the car seat, and maybe the stroller.

Or maybe not the stroller. Maybe fuck the stroller.

But the boy will need a visa or passport or however that'll work. I've only taken the very first steps toward proving he's entitled to dual citizenship. I hope I can finish sorting it out by the time my aunt has to head home, if she does come, maybe pay through the pee-hole for expedited processing if I can.

That brings me to the one thing that does give me pause, that keeps the thought of moving back to New Mexico from feeling like the massive relief that it frankly ought to.

And that's you.

I was too much of a coward to come out and say it the last time we spoke. I teased you with it. Teased us both with it.

But I love you.

Are you there, reading every one of these messages as they ping or buzz, I wonder?

I love you as much as one person who's never actually spoken aloud to the other person can. As much as somebody can love after just a couple weeks. As much as he can, based only on what the other person's chosen to reveal of herself.

But it's true. I love you, Maya.

And so leaving's going to hurt. So much worse than my body already does.

It seems like such a strange thing to hold me back. I mean, we've never even met. You're wherever my phone is.

Until my phone was suddenly gone, of course.

Not that it has to change anything, my going away. The time zones will be weird, but we've nearly always written like we were sending letters, haven't we? I hope you'll want to keep writing. There's not a lot waiting for me back home. The help of my aunt and hopefully my dad, maybe friends, maybe not. But I'll have you, still. I hope.

I hope.

Are you there? I don't think you are. I hope you're curled up watching a movie or going wrinkly in a lukewarm bath, lost in a book.

Anyhow. I've said a lot. My shoulder's sore from holding my good arm just so. The other one's screaming loud enough to drown out the painkillers, but only just now— for as long as I was writing to you,. it was silent. You've always been your own kind of magic.

I'm sorry for whatever you may have gone through when I disappeared on you. I hope you didn't worry too much. I hope you didn't doubt me, doubt us. I hope you weren't too sad or too angry. I wish I could protect you from anything that feels shitty, me with my shotgun laid across my lap, but I guess I can't.

The truth is, I'm not much use to anyone right now, and I won't be for a few months. Not until the shards strung through my arm start to resemble a bone again.

Hope to hear from you soon. That's about all I'm looking forward to, honestly. That and this new thing the boy does where he fetches my guitar and sets it carefully on the coffee table, then strums the strings, one at a time. That explodes my heart as well, but you...I miss you.

All the time I was stuck in the hospital, I'd think, this would be so much easier if I could just text her. The hours would've been so much shorter, the pain so much easier to take.

I missed you. I didn't miss whiskey, and I've been without that for a week, too. I only missed you.

Okay, I better go. Dinner's about ready. Later, stranger.

I hope.

TUESDAY

11.42am

Hello?

WEDNESDAY

10.19am

That was a long night. Every time I reached over to wake my phone, I'd tell myself I ought to just switch it off. Leave it until the morning.

Of course I didn't. Around four, I even got out of bed and stumbled around the kitchen, looking for the printout of my cell statement so I could double check the number. Even though I did that last night after dinner when I hadn't heard from you.

I wonder, did you see Private Number or Unknown Sender and ignore it?

Maybe, for a text or two.

But I sent fifty-six.

Surely that would've piqued your curiosity.

So I'm not really sure where I stand. I can only guess, and believe me, I've done little else for every second I've been conscious.

I wish I could see our texts, remember exactly what it was I last said to you. I was drunk. But only a little. Not enough to fuck things up that badly, I don't think. Though, then again, I'm not positive, either.

Did you text me after those final things we said? If it was all as perfect and sweet and horny and exhilarating as I think it was, you must have.

And I didn't text back.

Did you think I got spooked?

Did you think I regretted what I nearly wrote? I didn't. I only regret not writing it the moment I felt it.

Did you come to your senses, decide all of this was madness and pull the plug? Maybe you blocked my new number the same moment I reappeared.

Did none of this ever even happen at all? I could've dreamed it in the hospital, doped up on pain meds.

Except I've got that account statement, stranger. And you wouldn't believe how long that fucker is, that itemized proof of every time we've needed each other.

Did you maybe think it had all only ever been a creepy game, its objective to get a stranger to fall in love with me? Me, some bored sociopath, tapping out a depressing yarn to a random number in the middle of the night?

Or maybe you were playing that game. Maybe you were some dirty old man this whole time, getting off on pretending to be an innocent, a shut-in, the sweetest girl, saddled with the most heinous damage.

I don't think it's the last one. Whether it makes me a romantic or a fool, I want to believe you're exactly who you said you were. I want to believe that the woman I've fallen for is real, and that I played some small part in helping her find herself in that lonely flat, who knows where.

Because if she isn't real, and none of what I've felt these past few weeks has been real...I don't know where to go with that. I really don't.

Except, I suppose, back to the States.

THURSDAY

10.03pm

I was playing by our old rule, waiting until after ten. I told myself if I just showed some self-control and didn't check, I'd be rewarded. There you'd be, waiting, my message app stamped with a twelve or a thirty-two or a ninety-nine from all the messages you'd sent.

Messages saying, I'm so sorry, my battery was dead.

Saying, my ringer was off.

Saying, I was out. I was out, Malcolm, out in the world, at a bookstore, at a bakery, at an all-day movie marathon at the cinema. And you'd tell me how scary and wondrous and loud and smelly and glorious the outside is. Tell me about the velvet feel of running your fingers down the edges of new books, the way the honey glaze glistened, the heaven of real butter on movie theater popcorn. All this time, I'd have been trapped inside, you moving about your town or city a free woman. It would've been so poetic, inverted like that.

I think I'm going a little crazy. Or maybe it's the pills. I flit from moment to moment, leaping from one wild conclusion to another, hating myself for hurting you, or scaring you, abandoning you, letting you down. When I finish typing this, I'll hate myself for saying any of it, probably coming off unbalanced.

Are you there?

Even if you never want to hear from me again—please, just say so. Tell me to fuck off. It'd take so little time. Tell me now or make me grovel, if I've hurt you beyond forgiveness somehow. I'm sure I could have. I'm not the best person. I never have been.

Though I've been a better one with you. I've liked myself in a way I never truly had before. I've known myself, and been genuine as I never have been since I was a kid, probably.

You made me that man. Or you helped him come out. I want to be him. I want to stay this way, but I'm afraid I won't be able to without you.

So please reply. Please.

FRIDAY

3.34pm

Hi, stranger.

Or figment.

Fever dream.

Just thought I'd shout into the void. Call up out of the well, in case the sky felt like calling back.

Speaking of calling, I tried to call you. Just once. Didn't leave a message.

It went straight to voicemail, just some robot reading out your number. Does that mean it's switched off? Or that you blocked me? Maybe your battery's tapped, or you dropped your phone in the toilet by mistake. Maybe you're as frantic as I was when I was in the hospital, waiting for a replacement. To imagine the explanation is something like that…

Sometimes the hope is oxygen. Sometimes it's a slowly turning knife in my heart.

11.20pm

Hi, stranger.

Dear Diary.

I'm drunk. Not very—just a glass, except you really shouldn't mix it with the painkillers, and now I see why.

I'm on my own now with the boy. Lied to his grandma and told her I can cope, because her constant helpfulness was making me want to scream. I'd rather scald my good arm, fumbling with boiling pasta water, than have to sit through another meal with her.

The pain isn't making me a very grateful person. And the pills don't work the way they did at first.

The boy's paperwork is coming along, at least. There should be no problem getting him a U.S. passport. I already had the documentation from when the paternity was confirmed. I paid extra for rush processing. Once that comes, I'll book two plane tickets to Albuquerque. One-way.

Sometimes, I look out the window, and I'm surprised to think I'll actually miss that view. It hasn't rained in a week, and the village looks different when the sun shines. Maybe not quaint enough to be the backdrop for a spate of peculiar murders, but not far off.

Okay, I know you're not there. I get that it's pointless. I just wanted to write.

I'm lonely. And even your silence means more than talking to anyone who might pick up back home.

Sometimes, I even hear you whisper back. Snatches of words in a voice I can't quite hear, no matter how I strain. Like clutching at smoke.

I debate deleting your number, burning the account statement, culling all the messages I've sent since I got my new phone. I toy with telling myself it was all a hallucination and destroying the evidence that keeps me from believing that.

It'd be so sweet if that were true. So sweet to imagine it had never really been.

So I never really ruined it.

Goodbye, my love.

SATURDAY

8.02am

I told myself that hiding my phone in a room I never go in would mean it no longer existed, but I was just fooling myself about that. I had to go in after barely five days away from it— though, god, I didn't expect it to ping. Honestly, hearing that sound from a phone that should have been dead...it was like being electrocuted.

And of course I tried to play it cool, to not look, to do everything but check. I went to bed. I forced my eyes closed. I even made it as far as five in the morning.

But you should know by now that I couldn't resist forever.

Nor am I capable of pretending to be calm in this reply.

So I'm just going to go with what I want to most:

Oh my god, Malcolm. Malcolm. Are you still there?

Because I'm still here I'm here I'm so sorry I'm here. I thought you were the one who'd changed his mind, and then I was scared and I turned off the phone because it was so hard to look at that blank screen. It was killing me.

I can't believe it killed you too. But I should have known. I should have believed in you. Oh god, why didn't I believe? Now you're moving to some place I can barely pronounce with a terrible injury that I wasn't there to help you through and a broken heart that I accidentally passed from me to you like a pathogen from a zombie movie.

I should be quarantined for crimes against romance.

Malcolm, if you're there, please don't go. Don't do anything, okay? Just let me talk to you first—let me be all the things you were hoping I could be when you were laid up and lonely. I am those things, my love. I'm here for you emotionally. I can be more than here for you emotionally in fact. All I need you to do is answer this message.

8.33am

Maya, Jesus. Hi.

Hey, it's okay. Holy shit, I mean, it's more than okay. Don't feel bad. I don't blame you for hiding your phone away, if you felt even half as awful as I have since we fell out of touch.

Thank god. You're there. You're still there.

And you know you don't have to feel bad either, right?

At least you had good reason to suddenly stop messaging me.

That must have been a lot to take in. The news, but also… you know. What I said.

Wait, there I go being cagey about it again, after regretting it so much the first time. Fuck it—I love you. Let's put that right out there, once and for all.

You helped me dig myself out of the darkest episode of my life. You're amazing, and I love you, and it doesn't matter that we've never even met. And that we never will, now that I'm going back to the States.

Unless…

I dunno, unless you'd like me to come and see you before we go? I haven't booked the tickets yet, but I doubt I'll be here more than another two weeks.

It's just too hard, and I'm so fucking tired. I can't drive now, but I could pay for a cab. I don't know how far away you are, but it's not too far. There's no such thing as too far.

Would you like that? If I came to see you? To say hello, and then goodbye?

I don't think I could bear to say hello and then goodbye. But that's okay, because we don't have to. There doesn't have to be a goodbye if you don't want there to be. You don't need to come and see me. And you won't ever find things hard or be tired again, I promise. Just hold on. Wait, okay?

You're sweet, but it feels like I've already been holding on forever, honey. It's exhausting. I don't want to keep on struggling, wearing myself down and winding up back in the bottom of that well where you first found me.

And it's fine if you don't want to meet. I hope it wasn't too much to say. I understand how you are, and if that's how things need to be, I get it.

Shit, hang on. There's someone at the door.

I know, my Malcolm. I know.

It's me.

About Charlotte Stein

Charlotte Stein is the RT and DABWAHA nominated author of over fifty short stories, novellas and novels, including entries in *The Mammoth Book of Hot Romance* and *Best New Erotica 10*. When not writing deeply emotional and intensely sexy books, she can be found eating jelly turtles, watching terrible sitcoms and occasionally lusting after hunks.

charlottestein.net
facebook.com/charlottesteinauthor
twitter.com/charlotte_stein
charlotte_stein@hotmail.co.uk

About Cara McKenna

Since she began writing in 2008, Cara McKenna has published forty romances and erotic novels with a variety of publishers, sometimes under the pen names Meg Maguire and C.M. McKenna. Her stories have been acclaimed for their smart, modern voice and defiance of convention. She was a 2015 RITA Award finalist, a 2014 *RT* Reviewers' Choice Award winner, a 2012 and 2011 *RT* Reviewers' Choice Award nominee, and a 2010 Golden Heart Award finalist. She lives with her husband and son in the Pacific Northwest, though she'll always be a Boston girl at heart.

caramckenna.com
facebook.com/authorcaramckenna
twitter.com/caramckenna
cara@caramckenna.com

Also by Charlotte Stein

Raw Heat

Almost Real

Make Me

Closer

Giving

Reawakening

Ever Unknown

Lust Dazed

Guarded

The Horizon

Past Pleasures

Power Play

Waiting In Vain

The Things That Make Me Give In

Also by Cara McKenna

After Hours

Curio and the Curio Vignettes

Hard Time

Her Best Laid Plans

Shivaree: The Complete Series

Skin Game

Strange Love: Remastered Tales

Unbound

THE FLYNN AND LAUREL SERIES

Willing Victim

Brutal Game

THE DESERT DOGS SERIES

Lay It Down

Give It All

Drive It Deep

Burn It Up

Ride It Out

www.ingramcontent.com/pod-product-compliance
Lightning Source LLC
Chambersburg PA
CBHW051420170626
46809CB00006B/2244